I0707581

So Here We Are

Remembering

GRANDDADDY

So Here We Are

Brigadier General
Frederick Bates Butler
October 5th, 1896 – June 20th, 1987

Mary P. Henderson

So Here We Are

First Edition, June 2025

ISBN: 2370002059176 (paperback)

Library of Congress Control Number: 1-14929760071

Printed in the United States of America

Disclaimer
The information in this book is based on the author's research and experience. The author and publisher make no warranties, express or implied, regarding the accuracy or completeness of the content and are not liable for any damages arising from its use.

Cover Art by Rachel Bostwick

Dedication

For my siblings Chuck, Phil, Bob, and Kathy
And in loving memory to Mom.

And of course, to our Grandfather aka Granddaddy. A true war hero, successful leader, and blessed man. Always honoring and giving glory to God.
May he be remembered proudly with love.

Table of Contents

Frederic B. Butler

At West Point in 1918

Born	October 5, 1896
	San Francisco,

Preface

As a child, I saw him as a quiet, tall, dignified gentleman, stoic with a very powerful stable spiritual presence. Not intimidating but a larger-than-life aura nonetheless. Speaking laconically. Calm and peaceful unless provoked. Not much of a hugger.

I don't have many memories of my grandfather but the first and most dominating one that always comes to mind for me were the times that I spent sitting still and quietly, hands-clasped behind him in his third half-floor, book-lined library at his Seacliff San Francisco home, facing the back of his mahogany chair as he watched the evening news. I was careful not to make any noise. Listening to only the groaning of the fog horns as the famous fog rolled in and lapping Pacific ocean waves on the beach below.

I was young – probably 2, 4 and/or 6 years old - as my pregnant mom would drop me off to spend time with them at their Seacliff home prior to delivering one of my 3 younger brothers. The first time she walked me up those steep brick steps, rang the doorbell and handed me off to Grandmommy with my overnight bag. I stood confused - almost scared- in that high-beam ceiling, dark tiled foyer, watching my mom turn around and leave. Probably just an early bout of separation anxiety but as the heavy door closed, I ran to it pulling, yanking on the large wobbly crystal Victorian doorknob to open the heavy wood door to go after my mom but it wouldn't budge. I jerked it more to open it when Grandmommy came up from behind me, slapped my hand away, clearly irritated, raising her voice to me, saying tautly 'let me get that', and opened the door herself to allow me run down the stairs after mom. I caught her still in the driveway. By now I'm in tears so mom had me sit in the car while I gathered myself and then asking if I was ok, I nodded and said 'yes'. Probably only a couple of minutes. She said she would be back to get me soon, hugged me, told me to go back in, and drove off. I begrudgingly slowly walked up those brick steps again. Grandmommy was waiting for me at the top landing and then ushered me across the panel wood floors, past big ebony chests, with heavy brass grillwork, through the swinging door, to the big and roomy kitchen filled with interesting looking cupboards and drawers with blue and white Dutch china. There were black and white checkerboard marble tiled floors and there would be brownies and milk set out for me on the maids table next to a hissing radiator. I think there may have been a dog and a cat.

Around sunset every day, while I was there, Granddaddy would pull up a chair in front of his massive Mahogony desk, covered in loose pages, papers, periodicals and books, sitting tall and motionless yet posture-perfect within inches from his small 15" black and white TV perched on the edge of desk with his back to me, both of us facing the panoramic view of the Golden Gate Bridge over Baker Beach, sitting. In silence. Sometimes the sun was setting. Sometimes it was already set, dark outside and I'd hear the Pacific Ocean foghorn blowing over the San Francisco Bay. I can still smell the salty sea air of the incoming thick overnight fog.

He watched the evening news at the end of each day to follow the events of the world. CBSs' Walter Cronkite. ABC Huntley-Brinkley and probably the young journalist Peter Jennings as the ABC anchor later in the decade.

Maybe it was all the good books filling the three walls from floor to ceiling in the room or just his presence, but I would wander in to join him after putting away Grandmommy's antique dolls in their custom wardrobe cases back into the 2-single bed guestroom closet. I would silently climb the short half- set of stairs to join him when he was up there, grabbing an illustrated book off the wall-to-wall library shelves, grateful for the Peter Rabbit, Winnie the Pooh, and Charlotte Web books placed at my eye level on the lower shelf. The Wizard of Oz series covered one corner, books about California, maps, novels, and old, old books occupy another. There was a chaise lounge there for reading but I would sit on a small wooden straight-backed childrens chair they put out for me. The room was a small one and at night it was so cozy to sit up there under a cheery light and hear the lapping of the waves on the beach below, waiting for the famous San Francisco fog to roll in.

We would sit together in that study for as long as he wanted without saying a word to each other. Never any talking. But that was OK. At least he never baby-talked or talked down to me. But no hugs or kisses either. Altogether calm. Stillness. Peaceful times.

I liked it. It felt warm and safe to me. I wasn't uncomfortable. It's the room I would choose to sit in to stay out of Grandmommys way. She was most formal, requiring curtseys and thank you notes always. Taking me shopping for a hat at I Magnins in Union Square or feeding the ducks at the Palace of Fine Arts. Otherwise, I would wander down the stairs to the long and high-ceilinged living room, with thick, heavy crossbeams stretching across the ceiling. There was a beautiful deep and luxurious pale blue rug with a buff Chinese house in the center of it which matched the walls. There were hardly any knick knacks noticeable. This was the room with the huge bay window that looked directly at the Golden Gate Bridge like it was next door.

In front of the window, Grandmommy had her heavy, artistically carved, beautiful desk. A large fireplace was on one side of the room with a comfortable old couch facing it from the other side.

I could play with the old antique dolls stored in the guest room closets or wander the musky-and-wood polish smelling halls careful not to run into any of their domestic staff. Or I could sit in the clean chessboard black and white marble tiled floored kitchen where the cook would set out brownies and milk for me every afternoon. I did enjoy the treats of course but was jittery sitting in the small room at the small table off the giant dining room by myself. Afterall, I have always been a fidgety person by nature. Always moving fast. Mom said that's why my initials were 'MPH'. Miles per hour.

Granddaddy protected his well-earned solitude. Enjoyed the quiet.

Probably that was why he was so angry when our mischievous teenage cousin Derek pulled the burglar alarm in the alcove coat closet that Christmas Eve when we were all celebrating the holidays at their beautifully decorated home. I think it was pre-dinner cocktail hour, causing a surprise rare chaos, a blast of sirens filled the air, unleashing confusion and Granddaddy's temper. He was so angry but now I can now understand the reaction, most likely triggered from his war years, loud bombings, air raid blasts, etc. It sensitizes a person.

His nephew said he hated politics. And the limelight.   There was a story about him meeting with reporters when he retired from San Francisco International Airport as General Manager in 1960. There was a press conference and he said absolutely nothing.

He was a devout catholic; he went to communion every morning. He held Christian values, stemming the tide of evil, upholding family and preservation of life.

According to his nephew Lewis, he disliked FDR. Probably some of it stemmed from his witnessing firsthand the disrespectful transfer of presidential power from his friends, the Hoovers in 1933 after Roosevelt's landslide victory; FDR treated the Hoovers very poorly during that transition. Or maybe because one of the first things Mr. Roosevelt did after taking office in his first administration was to take away Public Buildings and Parks from the jurisdiction of the Assistant Secretary of War and transfer it to the Interior Department. Probably not an issue though since Granddaddy agreed publicly that that was probably a more logical place for it. But I have since learned, that as Army Corp of Engineers in charge of the White House facility - that he was responsible for all the physical improvements required at the White House, including for the accommodations for the wheelchair-bound, handicapped, new President FDR and they were all to be installed in a 2-hour window on the day the Hoovers moved out in the morning and the Roosevelts moved in after the parade and before the crowded reception in the afternoon. After the parade, there were so many people rushing the White House for food and refreshments – all had proper invitations – that they had run out of food and Granddaddy had to break away from presenting people to Mrs. Roosevelt to tell staff to break out the reserves and call every caterer in Washington. Years later, when accompanying Roosevelt in his motor car who was receiving an honor at a formal military review, Granddaddy remembered enjoying a quite cordial and relaxed, light-hearted exchange of fond memories with FDR about that inauguration day. Roosevelt greeted him fondly, saying "'Oh, Lieutenant, we miss you so much." and somehow or other they got talking about that Inaugural Day situation, and Granddaddy said "you know, Mr. President after that experience I know what they mean when they say,' a hungry democrat'. FDR threw back his head and they both laughed So perhaps bygones were bygones.

Granddaddy was an American World War II General through and through.

He served in the North African, Italian and French campaigns, including the invasion of Southern France where with an armored column under his command called "Task Force Butler" capturing 2,000 to 3,000 Germans, while suffering only 15 casualties. He led Task Force Butler successfully into [1]the Battle of Montelimar, winning the Distinguished Service Cross, the Legion of Merit and the Bronze Star.

General Lucian Truscott, his commander in Italy and Southern France - one of the most decorated generals of WWI and WWII with a career spanning 30 years, including replacing General Patton (after his politically incorrect rants), called Granddaddy **'one of the most fearless men'** he had ever met after assigning him to lead an ad hoc group of poorly-supplied but experienced soldiers behind enemy lines on the Italian battlefield during World War II.

In the October 1965 Ignatian Bulletin, as he was awarded the Christ the King' Award, at his high school alum mater, it was printed in the program that *"From 1921 to 1953, 'General Butlers life was strictly Army'.*

Retired General Butler deservedly to be addressed as either 'General'. Or 'Sir'. Except for us. His Grandchildren. We called him 'Granddaddy'.

———

Prologue

Nearly a decade after Granddaddy passed away, my financial company was selected as a co-managing bond underwriter on a $106 million San Francisco Airport (SFO) Special Facility 1997 Lease Revenue Bond Issue. As my firm's lead managing investment banker, I attended all the finance team meetings held in the administrative offices on the 3rd floor at San Francisco Airport to work on the deal structure and negotiate the financing terms. As the only woman in the room and surrounded at the conference room table by all male investment bankers in blue suits and power ties from Smith Barney, airport and bond consultants, and the Airports finance officers, as well as top national legal bond counsels, I was surprised to discover Granddaddy's large, framed portrait ceremoniously hanging on the boardroom wall amongst all the other previous general managers, staring at me, drawing my attention momentarily away from the meeting.

Afterall, I knew only that he had been in the War - not in such a high executive position here at the Airport, wondering if he was also then responsible for Butler Field naming rights too (which he wasn't). I couldn't help but wonder what else I did not know about him. Trying hard to stay focused on my task at hand, I had to compartmentalize those questions for another time. Yet I felt so proud; I sat a little taller. I couldn't shake his presence with me in that windowless, crowded room that long, tedious day.

After the meeting, I mentioned it casually while shaking hands at the end of the day-long meeting with the current Airport General Manager and seemed to gain a new tacit respect from him and acceptance from all around the table from thereon. Already overwhelmed with all the moving parts of this complicated bond issue, as well as struggling to not be considered just a token WBE hire, I told myself I would think more about it later. Later, when I had some time to talk to my Mom more about him.
Afterall, I only knew him as my grandfather. And that he was a general in the War. Stories were never shared.
But I never got the chance to have this conversation with my Mom. I was too busy and she died of cancer.

And now, I finally have time to research and reflect...

So here we are.

Figure 1 Granddaddy, General Manager of SFO

Figure 2 SFO Offering document

Introduction

This story is my humble attempt to share with you – my siblings - what I have learned over the past year about our maternal grandfather. It's truly remarkable. We should all feel so proud.

Since other than some Christmas gatherings memories, we don't really have any stories about him - and with Mom gone too - I began to research on my own.

Jumpstarted by a written Lewis Butler interview that Chuck shared with me, I started putting together a collection of mostly hearsay, Google research, a couple of published war books from the internet and the local library, and some random notes that miraculously have survived over 100 years - so that our grandfathers' selfless bravery, his memory and our DNA history will not get lost or ever forgotten.

But like most quick projects that lead you down a rabbit hole of information, I found more and more references to him, especially during World War II in the memoirs of his commanders that confirm his bravery, courage, sense of humor, loyalty and love of country.

So here we are.

The fear. The terror. His courage. Bravery. Strength. The war horrors he experienced and witnessed; the sacrifices he made, the pain he endured so that we can have the freedoms we enjoy today.

I am most grateful and honored to call him my grandfather; I doubt I can do his story justice. But it's a start.

And to my brothers and sister, always remember, that much of the abundance we all enjoy is simply where God put us in our family line, reaping what they have sowed.

God has been working for us behind the scenes for generations. Some of the favor we see, has nothing to do with us, it's the goodness of God, putting the right people in our lives.

Because he lived a life of integrity and service and honored God, he put us in a position to be blessed. It is a reminder (from me) that his blessings he gave us walk within us now.

We are reaping from what our relatives have sowed.

Something for everyone.   Besides the Generals' Army career across the globe during World War II, I've included interesting side stories and connections with other Butlers here too i.e., his sister-in-law and our Great Aunt Lucy, his nephew Lewis, Golf, Pasatiempo, Stanford, President Hoover, Yosemite, a little history (Mom would have liked that), including World War II, and the Bohemian Club. But of course, most of his story is from the U.S. Army. He was all about the Army.

Enjoy!

An Overview
Frederick Bates Butler

Frederick Bates Butler, was born in San Francisco, California on October 5, 1896, as son of Vincent Kingwell Butler (1864-1933) and Mary L. Flynn (1864-1929). His father had immigrated from Kilkenny Ireland during the potato famine. He had two older brothers.

He attended St. Ignatius High School College Preparatory, a Jesuit school in San Francisco where he graduated from in 1913. He attended University of San Francisco for three years in civil engineering then was a cadet at the United States Military Academy at West Point, New York, from June 15, 1916, to November 1, 1918 as an appointment from the State of California.

Upon graduation in 1918, he was promoted in the Army to 2nd lieutenant Corps of Engineer. He served in China & Outer Mongolia with Army Corps of Engineers (ACE) and taught at West Point before returning to San Francisco in 1929. Still in service, he worked on Treasure Island 1939-40 after the World Fair and became directly responsible for design and construction of Treasure Island landfill and Yerba Buena roadway for the 1939-40 Golden Gate International Exposition before Treasure Island was sold to the U.S. Navy for Pacific War Theatre base.

He married Philippi Harriette Harding in Tientsin, China on November 12, 1924. They would have two daughters, Patricia M. Butler (born 1927) and Phillipa "Popsy" Butler (born 1935), and one son William Butler (born August 28, 1928).

From 1921 to 1953, his life was strictly Army. For 4 years, he was a Brigadier General during WWII.

In World War II, he was involved in both the African campaign as G-3 in the Advance Headquarters, II Corps, in Tunisia 1943, in Italy being promoted Colonel commander 168th Infantry Regiment and the invasion of Southern France, where as Brigadier General in VI Corps he led Task Force Butler into the Battle of Montelimar.

While in the Army, he earned 8 awards and medals and had 7 promotions 1918-1944.

He retired for physical disability in 1953; he returned home wounded.

He died June 20th, 1987.

Chapter 1:
Somewhere in France
(August 22, 1944)

"The Germans were probing everywhere. Early in the afternoon we got a real scare. Five Mark tanks, supported by panzer grenadiers succeeded in crossing the Roubion near Cleon. Troop A fought skillfully, knocking out several of the supporting vehicles, but became cut off and surrounded. The Germans even worked into (the Town) of Puy St. Martin, where (Lieutenant Colonel Joseph G.) Felber had his headquarters. This was the time and place to use my reserves and, anticipating enemy power in the area, this was the location. I had picked out from which the reserve was to operate. But the slowness of the relief at the Gap had delayed this vital element of the command. It was still on the road. The tank destroyers that Felber had did excellent work and stemmed the advance. More power was needed. One platoon of Troop A still was cut off and had lost two armored cars and three jeeps. Due to the hilly nature of that country we could not raise our advancing column by radio. Its commanding officer had driven ahead and was at the CP. Now the Germans were between us and his troops. He estimated the column could not be more than thirty minutes from the point where they would contact the enemy. Forewarned would be forearmed. Our

only chance of communication was a dropped message from a cub. An artillery plane was called in, given the message, dropped it, and our rescue columns arrived for a movie finish. The German tanks which had crossed the Roubion were destroyed, the infantry were driven back and on the south bank, several fires burned merrily where our guns had found trucks and light vehicles. It was a good honest fight. The reserve had arrived in the nick of time."

by Brigadier General Frederic B. Butler
Task Force Butler, 1946

Chapter 2:
Before the War

First, to get started, let me tell you a little about Granddaddy in his early years.

Butler Family

He was the youngest of three boys. A native of San Francisco, California. U.S.A.

His oldest brother was Raymond Butler who became a Jesuit priest.

Then there was Vincent. In 1923, Vincent married Lucy Hanchett Butler (Born November 24th, 1899), a daughter of a gold miner and land developer, Lewis Hanchett. She was educated at the Katherine Delmar Burke School in San Francisco, Mis Ransom's School in Piedmont and Miss Bennett's College in Millbrook, N.Y. As a young woman, Granddaddys' sister-in-law (our great aunt Lucy) was an accomplished athlete, competing statewide in tournaments in tennis and golf.

His brother Vincent (our great uncle), a World War I veteran, attended St, Ignatius College (now the University of San Francisco) and graduated from as a Rhodes scholar from Oxford University in 1914. He became a very successful San Francisco attorney, representing Standard Oil and celebrities like the leading woman golfer Marion Hollins.

Lucy, a socially prominent San Franciscan, always thought that the eldest brother Raymond should have been a bartender not a Jesuit priest, and that Granddaddy should have been a Jesuit priest because he was such a holy guy.

Lucy used to give Raymond a bottle of whiskey when he came to visit, and they had a charade that the whiskey was for one of the older Jesuits who'd been ill and could use a little drink.

His brother Vincent and sister-in-law Lucy

While Granddaddy was training for the war across the country and on overseas assignments such as mapping terrain in China, his brother Vincent and his family – his wife Lucy, and sons Vincent Butler Jr. and Lewis Hanchett Butler - living in San Francisco, would go down to Aptos on most weekends; the family would be at the beach all summer long and spend a couple a weeks a year in Yosemite. Vincent would also be at the Bohemian Club, and at the Family Club. His son Vincent Jr. would later say about his Dad, '*He was an Irish kid who wanted to be somebody in town, and he was somebody.*'[2] He was in line to be the president of the Bohemian Club and to this day on the fourth floor of the Bohemian Club there's a big bas relief plaque, not so big, with Vincents' name on it. In his memory. Forty-two years old.

Yosemite was also always a big deal in Vincents' family's lives. Even in the middle of the Depression. For Vincent, who had a good job, there was always plenty of money around and time to do things. They'd go to Yosemite in the days when there would be

---

2 Tapes

snow in Yosemite Valley. They skijored, where you skied behind a horse and ride around in a sleigh in Yosemite Valley. Back then they didn't have enough money to stay at the Ahwahnee Hotel but stayed at the lodge and had a little cabin, 22-C, that years later, when after Vincent later died, the family always went back to, to go skiing. And Lucy would give out the little trophy for the junior skiers. They'd also be there in Yosemite a lot for the summer.

For two weeks or a month, Vincent Jr. and Lewis would be put in the Yosemite Little Grizzly Club, which was basically babysitting, so Lucy could go have a good time. They'd take them out and teach them nature courses and all that kind of stuff. And as they got older, they'd get to hike up to little Yosemite, over Vernal and Nevada Falls. I don't know what they did when they were six or seven. I guess they did whatever you do at that age. I don't think they went hiking. Lucy loved to ride and was a good rider, so she'd go off on a horse, on trails. But also in those days, they'd play tennis at the Ahwahnee Hotel tennis court. And she'd go fishing. She was a very good fisherperson. Left-handed caster. She was ambidextrous. And she had a lot of friends. And then in the winter, they skied. And at that time, she was getting to know Mary Curry Tresidder who ended up as her closest friend when they were both widows after the war. She met her while visiting Yosemite.

As a side note, Mary's parents David and Jennie founded Curry Village, welcoming guests to Yosemite in 1899. They started the Yosemite Park and Curry Company and pushed out all their competitors. And Mary's husband, Don Tresidder, was running the company in those days. Marys' friends were sort of in the higher echelon in the early days; She was the hostess at the Ahwahnee Hotel. It was very much a kind of precious little group of people, because not everybody could afford to go to Yosemite in the depths of the Depression.

Pasatiempo

Around 1927, while Granddaddy was busy teaching at West Point before the war, Vincent and Lucys' friend Marion Hollins, the Country's women's golf champion[3], horsewoman and "It Girl", was selling real estate for Pebble Beach and she helped lay out the golf course that's now Cypress Point. Probably the most famous 3-par hole in America, if not the world, is its' sixteenth hole.

Marion was a big woman. Later one of the great women golf stars said she was just a big bundle of Scottish clothes, basically tweeds. Just this huge bundle of tweeds that would wind up and hit the ball a mile. Out there on the ocean she tees up a ball and hits it across this 200-yard expanse and that becomes this famous sixteenth hole at Cypress Point at Pebble Beach, which is still a private course. The architect was Alistair McKenzie, the great golf course architect who eventually designed the famous Masters course in Cypress Point, Augusta National Golf Course in Georgia, and the Pasatiempo course in Santa Cruz.

McKenzie also collaborated in the design of many other lesser-known California courses including Meadow Club in Marin County (1927), the remodeling of the Pebble Beach golf links

---

3 She was finally admitted to the World Golf Hall of Fame in 2022

14

(1927-28), the Valley Club of Montecito in Santa Barbara County, the magical 9-hole Northwood Golf Course along the Russian River and its majestic redwood trees near the Bohemian Grove in Sonoma County (1928), and Green Hills Golf Club in Millbrae (1930). He went on to design courses in Australia, South America and New Zealand.

It was during the Depression that Marion took all her share of some oil money and spent it all buying the ranch in Pasatiempo and had her friend Alistair McKenzie design the golf course—still one of the hundred most famous golf courses in America. She had her own house on the golf course, and then she gave Lucy and Vincent the two-acre lot next door on the fifth hole, selling it to them for a thousand bucks or something. Lucy and Vincent hired this promising young architect, Bill Wurster, and he designed a wonderful summer house for them called Four Corners—still a famous house, now destroyed. and the house is just about finished when Vincent boards a United Airlines flight to the East Coast probably as the firm's Standard Oil attorney.

Marion died broke on August 27th, 1944 in Pacific Grove at 51 years old while Grandaddy would be finishing up his most triumphant war operation of his career, commanding Task Force Butler in southern France According to his Commander General Truscott (more on all that later), without Granddaddys' Task Force speed of execution and heroic pursuit of the enemy, 'we would not have been able to gain the rear of the German XIX

Army at Montelimar,'4   which considerably hindered the Germans escape, pushing back their lines of defense.

So it was back in 1935 that Granddaddy's brother Vincent had a choice of flying instead of four days on the train, and of course flying then meant you took off from San Francisco, landing in Reno; then you went from Reno to Salt Lake City, Salt Lake City to Cheyenne, Cheyenne to Omaha, or wherever; and about twenty hours later, it got you to the East Coast. So he had a choice of taking United Airlines, one of those Boeing twin engine planes or an identical plane owned by Standard Oil. He decided for whatever reason to fly on the United Airlines plane. It was being flown by the crack pilot for United Airlines. It was a routine night flight, going into Cheyenne but miscalculated, and the plane hit a hill outside of the Cheyenne Airport and killed everybody. It was October 7, 1935. That same night the Standard Oil airplane also had some malfunction and crashed in Salt Lake, killing everybody. His son Lewis would later call it 'a bizarre coincidence'.

So now Lewis and Vincent had no father. Lucy became devoted to raising and educating her two sons.

Lucy's brother Nelson and Granddaddy would step in as much as possible over the years to be a substitute father for his brothers' son Vincent. He was 'Uncle Fred'. When Vincent was older,

---

4 Command Missions Lucian K. Truscott, page 349

Granddaddy would take him to Bohemian Grove as his guest and have him join him in Texas as he was training some new recruits; His brother Raymond would take Vincent to the Santa Clara-USF-St. Mary's football games and so on.

Meanwhile, also on March 3, 1935, earlier that year, Granddaddys' youngest daughter, Phillipi, was born and he was stationed at West Point New York. Others would call her 'Popsy'. We called her 'Mom'.

Figure 3 Popsy Butler –

Inscribed "With all love to her godmother Marian from Phillippa Butler" December 1937 (2yrs 9 mos)

After Vincents death, his family would still go every summer to Pasatiempo and live in that house, and Lewis learned to play golf, making money caddying, They grew up during those Depression years on the Pasatiempo golf course in the summer, and then during the war it was rented to an army officer and finally it was sold.

Their family would spend the week in San Francisco and then get into their Buick with Nellie the cook, and maybe a friend each for the boys, and drive to Santa Cruz down Bayshore on the undivided four-lane highway with only a double yellow line to block oncoming traffic and dangerous intersections, turn off at Sunnyvale at the Moffett Field, driving to Cupertino and Saratoga, Los Gatos, and over the hill, getting carsick on the winding road until they put in Highway 17, which was the big modern highway, a death trap still to this day. That's why they called it the "bloody Bayshore'.

Lucy was an involved parent. She was a very good athlete—she'd played catcher on the boys' baseball teams. Her sons were both good athletes and she had them taught to play golf and tennis. They'd get hand-me-down Wimbledon rackets from her friend Helen Wills (the celebrity top female tennis champion in the World for eight years) that she didn't need any longer. She'd play baseball with them, and up to the time Lewis was fourteen or fifteen years old—he could throw as hard as he could at his mother and she'd catch it with this big catcher's mitt.

And since Lucy was a skier, she would continue to take her sons to Yosemite starting in the late thirties, and she gave the little ski trophy for the kids' ski races. She loved to fly fish and go camping with them. Up to the time Lewis was thirteen years old, he went camping with his mother and two other people, a packer and a great fisherman friend of hers, for two weeks in Yosemite when they didn't see one other party for a couple of weeks. They packed into the back country, hiked the scenic granite cliffs and creeks of the 41.6 mile loop trail Jack Main Canyon and up towards the northern boundary of Yosemite Park in 1940. Lucy loved to ride horses; she'd always ridden. She was a wonderful mother for boys.

Lucy and her family were always financially comfortable since following Vincents tragic death, she had been advised by Vincents professional friends to file a wrongful death claim against the airline. There really wasn't any wrongdoing with the aircraft or the pilot but a wrongful death claim was filed against United Airlines[5] anyway and they paid it. The amount was about $75,000 or so but that was a lot of money back then; It was awarded right in the middle of the Depression in 1935. Her advisors told her that Standard Oil was part of a consortium to find oil in Saudi Arabia, and they hadn't drilled the first well yet, but they were very optimistic, so they bought Standard Oil stock with most of the money. Of course, the consortium would soon find oil in Saudi Arabia. Lucy owned that stock until the day she died, and I read that the basis of the stock was about 30 cents and it was worth maybe eighty or 100 bucks a share. So basically, Lucy lived on that money for the rest of her life. So that, financially, saved the family.

She was active in the Junior League and the Town and Country Club of San Francisco and was a board member of the San Francisco Children's Theater while also serving as a director of the Yosemite Park & Curry Co.

---

5 Vincents' Law firm had to transfer their client, United Airlines, to Brobeck, Phleger & Harrison, which was probably the second biggest firm back then. The Phlegers were friends of theirs and lived around the corner.

Later she lived five blocks away from her boys in San Francisco, so when Lewis finally got back from school and had a family, Vincents wife and Lewis took care of her. In 1952, she lived in a beautiful apartment not far from our Grandparents Seacliff home.

She would die at home at the age of 94.

His Nephew Lewis Butler

In Lewis' Own Words

'He (Uncle Fred) was a General, and he had all the great characteristics of a wonderful, wonderful army officer and all the other characteristics – discipline; went to Mass every morning; went to communion every morning; hated killing people; captured a whole German army because he didn't want to kill them. A wonderful man but he was a General to the core.'
-Lewis Butler, 2009

Bohemian Club

Granddaddys nephew Lewis (Lucy and Vincents son) became a member of the Bohemian Club because he liked to go there with his two 'fathers', aka Lucy's brother Uncle Nelson and his 'Uncle Fred'. But it irritated Lewis more and more that they wouldn't take Jews and they certainly wouldn't take blacks. So he finally quit when he was in the federal government.

He wrote to both Granddaddy and Nelson, saying, "Dear revered ones, I'm quitting and part of it is because you guys are getting old and you don't go as much anymore, but also frankly, I just can't stand the policies of the place."

Granddaddy basically wrote back saying, "Well, maybe you should stay in and try to change the place from inside," which Lewis found absurd for some strange reason.

Granddaddy said, "Stay inside and maybe you could change something", and Uncle Nelson wrote him "I'm willing to support you in whatever you do even if it means living up to your own ideals".

So Lewis quit the Club.

Lewis graduated from Princeton and went to Stanford Law School; he became an attorney and as forever a peace activist and a self-proclaimed environmental politician, he went on to achieve great things, including as Head of the Peace Corps Malysia, U.S. Asst. Secy of department of Health Education and Welfare, establishing and leading numerous nonprofits and foundations. His California Law Firm of Butler & McCloskey three biggest deals were the BCDC Save the Bay, the Napa Valley, and the Dos Rios Dam.

Later, Herb Caen would try to get Lewis to consider running for Mayor against Joe Alioto. So he came to see Granddaddy at his Sea Cliff home since he had been head of the San Francisco Airport when they moved Mills Field out to what's now SFO.

(While he was in the U.S. Corps of Engineers, the manager of the Airport had quit. Since he knew quite a bit about city hall, he took that job. He was a terrible politician but was seen as a wonderful man of unbelievable integrity.)

So anyway, after Granddaddy retired, Lewis visits him at his Sea Cliff home and Granddaddy tells him "Do you really want to get involved with city hall? That's a tough place."

He didn't say not to do it. But by the time Lewis got to the dinner, he'd decided it was a really bad idea, and he even said later "I just had the fat head and was flattered and all that."

Frederick B. Butler (1896-1987)

Let's talk more about Granddaddy. 'Grandaddy was all Army'[6]

His Army Career (1921-1953)

Frederick B. Butler was an Army man through and through. He was stationed all over the world, including but not limited to, New York, Virginia, Oklahoma, Los Angeles, Kansas, North Africa, France, Italy, South Korea, Australia and Japan.

Summary of Promotions

- *Second Lieutenant November 1, 1918*
- *First Lieutenant May 7, 1919*
- *Captain November 1, 1934*
- *Major July 1, 1940*
- *Lieutenant Colonel September 15, 1941, accepted September 22, 1941*
- *Colonel February 1, 1942*
- *Brigadier General January 17, 1944*

West Point Cadet USMA (1916-1918)

After graduating from San Francisco Jesuit School in 1913, he went to West Point, New York, graduating from United States Military Academy West Point in 1918, ranking 8th in his class.

---

[6] Lewis Butler Tapes

Second Lieutenant (1918 - 1919)

He was promoted in the Army to Second Lieutenant, Corps of Engineers. He served at Camp A. A. Humphreys in Virginia as student officer at Engineer School, from December 2, 1918, to June 1919. He was then sent to France with American Expeditionary Forces, on a tour of observation, to September 1919.

Figure 4 Harding Butler wedding Notice 1924 in her hometown of Los Angeles

First Lieutenant (1919 – 1935)

He graduated from Camp A. A. Humphreys to the United States Army Engineer School in 1921 and spent a couple of months at the Fort Sill Oklahoma Field Artillery School before traveling to Tientsin China in January 1923 where he was Aide-de-camp to Commanding General U.S. Army Forces in China under Brigadier General William D. Connor for three years in China.

Wedding (1924)

His soon-to-be, 25-year-old, wife Phillippi Harriete Harding (aka Grandmommy) traveled to China and they were married in St. Louis

Church in Tientsin in China on November 12th, 1924 when he was stationed in Tientsin as aide to Major General Fox Connor. General Connor and his wife hosted their wedding celebration. Grandmommy lived two years in China with him while he was working there. They lived at 29 Tungehow Road Tien-Tsin.

Phillippi Harriete Harding Butler (1899 – 1984)

Not to be outdone as impressive, especially for the times, Grandmommy had an extraordinary college and career experience, especially for a bright young woman in the early 1900's.

Born in Chicago, growing up in Los Angeles, she was the daughter of Mr. and Mrs. William Alfred Harding. She was a brilliant student at Stanford in a day when women didn't go to college. She graduated with a PhD from Stanford in 1920 **Phi Beta Kappa in mathematics** in 1920 and was a member of the Delta Delta Delta sorority.

She began working as a secretary to the wife of Herbert Hoover while the future president and his wife Lou were still living on the Stanford campus. When the Hoovers went to Washington in 1920, she went with them, living with the Hoovers in D.C. while Hoover was Secretary of Commerce, serving under Harding (and after Harding's death in 1923, President Calvin Coolidge.)

She was Miss Harding at the time. She met Granddaddy there when he was a lieutenant. She lived with the Hoover family and was a member of the household at 2300 S Street. Granddaddy later said he 'was on duty at one of the military posts near Washington at the time and, through normal social gyrations,

24

became acquainted with Miss Harding. 'So you can see, our romance goes back further than the White House'[7].

He ended up by taking her out of the Hoover establishment in 1924, and she traveled out to China where he was then on duty. He always chuckled – he said, 'she chased me all the way out to China and arrived with the ring'.

Mapping China (1923-26)

In 1925, Granddaddy was 1st Lieutenant Butler cartographer with U.S. Army Corps of Engineers (ACE), working as a 3-member topographic team as assistant topographer on the Third Asiatic Expedition in Tianjin (Tientsin) China, leaving Peking (Beijing) China for Outer Mongolia April 11, 1925 with Roy Chapman Andrews. His research focused on fossil hunting and exploring the region and were well known not merely in the field of paleontology, but geological and mineralogical as well. Andrew's work in Outer Mongolia, particularly in the Gobi Desert, yielded significant discoveries, including dinosaur eggs, early examples of Oviraptor and Protoceratops, and the first evidence that dinosaurs laid eggs.

The Roy Chapman Andrews expedition headed to Outer Mongolia, traveling a couple of days ahead of the rest of the expedition to conduct surveys of the area, recording the route taken and locating interesting scientific places while interacting with Mongolian natives and taking note of changing political

____

7 Hoover interview

times until returning to Tiensin in August 1925. They had camels for their pack train and relief-supplies but personally traveled in motor-trucks. Granddaddy returned home with many artifacts, treasures, and collectables, including a fragmented piece of a dinosaur eggshell, hand carved chests, rosewood chairs, and low inlaid tables.

He would recall later, when taping an interview about the Hoovers, that he was asked about his experiences in Mongolia since Mr. Hoover had also spent some time in his mining days in the Far East, prospecting in Mongolia in the early 1900's. Granddaddy wasn't sure that he didn't have the facilities that they had, or the varied personnel that they had with them, but yet Hoovers' conclusions as to the mineral situation were just about the same as the conclusions that came out of their expedition decades later.

In other words, the two expeditions – if you can call Mr. Hoover's little group an expedition – came up with just about the same conclusion as to what Mongolia was, what the geological situation was, what the mineral prospects were, and so forth. He saw with his naked eye and felt with his bare hands and came up with the same results as the highly organized group of scientists decades later. And these 2 expeditions were about 25 years apart, but, as Mr. Hoover was on pony back or had only camels for transportation, Granddaddy's group traveled in motor vehicles.

Teaching and Publishing (1926-27)

From 1926-27, Granddaddy was an instructor in the Department of Tactics and with Engineer detachment at the United States

Military Academy at West Point, publishing many articles on my map work, giving lectures, and teaching until the early 30's when he would join the Hoover White House after working in the San Francisco office for the United States Corp of Engineers.

The Hoover White House (1930 -1933)

While still in the Corps of Engineers, he 'somehow was given the responsibility for the White House during the Hoover Administration'.

The Hoover Connection

As already mentioned, there was an earlier connection with the Hoover family and our Grandparents.

Grandmommy worked as a personal secretary for Lou Henry Hoover while she was a senior at Stanford University. When the Hoovers went to Washington D.C. in 1920, she went with them while Hoover was Commerce Secretary. Then she became First Lady Lou Hoover's personal private secretary in the White House and oversaw responding to pleas for assistance during the Great Depression[8].

Meanwhile in 1930, having spent twelve years of commissioned service, Granddaddy became Assistant Director of Public Buildings and Parks in the District of Columbia. Mr. Hoover

---

8 Wanna know more? Sorry but mom said Aunt Pat 'destroyed all Grandmommy's papers and letters which Grandma Harding had kept all that time'.

would refer to him as a White House aide, but he never was. He took care of many public buildings, and of course, the White House is a public building and though not the largest of his responsibilities in size, it demanded more attention than all the other things put together. He was a First Lieutenant; A Lieutenant sixteen years to the day. There were only about 125,000 men in the whole Army back then.

He had a lot of direct contact with Mrs. Hoover too, especially during her remodeling projects. 'She was a person who definitely knew what she wanted, there were no ands, ifs or buts. She knew how to get what she wanted and she wasn't happy until she got what she wanted. With it all, she was most gracious, thoroughly ladylike and thoroughly considerate', he said later in the 1967 Hoover interview.

He said she had some excellent ideas for improving the White House. No structural changes were started by the Hoovers but the completion of the remodeling of the top floor of the White House was accomplished during their residency and as for the main floor and the second floor, Mrs. Hoover did a great deal. A great deal of the work that was done out of the Hoovers own personal finances. Only the draperies were at public expense.

They did a lot of the work on the family floor over a weekend. As soon as they got the frame out for some new recessed shelving Mrs. Hoover wanted, they ran into heavy brick; not walls — buttresses, and some burnt wood from remnants of the building burning in 1814.

Rapidan Camp

Our grandparents became very close with the Hoovers. Granddaddy's contact with Mr. Hoover would be termed 'mostly social' however they occasionally had serious discussions.

Our Grandparents would accompany the Hoovers as guests to the Rapidan Camp on the weekends, nestled in the Blue Ridge Mountains, 100 miles from Washington. Some thought he was there in a U.S. Army capacity but Camp Rapidan was strictly a Marine stronghold.

Rapidan Camp or "Camp Hoover" in Shenandoah National Park in Virginia was bought and built by the Hoovers at a delightful cooler location at the headwaters of the Rapidan with an elevation of about 1500 feet. Mrs. Hoover laid out and superintended the construction of a series of log cabins to accommodate only 12 – 15 guests. It was 100 miles from White House and connected by a single direct telephone. It was the historic summer camp of President Herbert Hoover and First Lady Lou Henry Hoover, serving as their rustic retreat throughout his administration (1929-1933).

Friday afternoons, the Hoovers would leave the White House by car and head to Rapidan; A 2nd car with Secret Service, a 3rd car with newspaper reporters and a 4th with guests would follow. A 5th car containing supplies and luggage would bring up the rear.

Mr. Hoover was a big fly fisherman and built several pools along the upper Rapidan canyon, turning it into a successful trout stream. Granddaddy gave fly rods to Aunt Lucy for the boys that had belonged to the Hoovers.

During Washington's exhausting summer heat, they spent a lot of weekends with the Hoovers at Rapidan camp as their guests gathered around the fireplace in the building or on the porch. Everybody was at ease there; there was no formal meeting atmosphere. There was always a particular group there; Rarely any repeats.

At the end of Hoovers term, he presented the land and the camp to the Park Service for the future use of the White House or alternatively to the Boy and Girls Scout organizations. Grandmommy and two of her friends went to Rapidan four weeks after Hoover was defeated in the election and began the sad task of packing up belongings.

After Hoover lost the election, he came back to Stanford. So would Granddaddy and Grandmommy.

Our grandparents stayed in touch with the Hoovers, visiting with Mr. Hoover in Palo Alto, receiving thoughtful notes from them both for many family events throughout the years.
When Granddaddys brother Vincent died in the plane crash, Mrs. Hoover sent Lucy a lovely note of condolences. It basically said,

'this is so sad, your father was a wonderful man', handwritten, Lou Henry Hoover.

As it turned out, Herbert Hoover—of course this was when he was an ex-president in 1935—was supposed to be on the plane that crashed, killing Granddaddy's brother, but then at the last minute didn't go.

For their youngest daughter Popsy's wedding years later in 1956, The Hoovers sent autographed copies of his 3-volume set of his memoirs to them as a wedding gift, inscribed with:

"To Philippa and Robert Henderson – The good wishes of Herbert Hoover. For yours the greatest adventure in life'

'The affection which was your mothers when she understood the same adventure',

and for the volume entitled "The Great Depression 1929-1941", he signed it as

'This is a dull book about a bad time but your mother lived it also – Herbert Hoover.'

Captain (1934-1940)

Then while at U.S. Miliary Academy, Mom (Phillipa "Popsy" Butler) was born at West Point, New York in 1935, joining her two siblings. Older brother Bill (William H.) was 7 years old; Older Sister Pat (Patricia B. Reardon) was 6 years old or as we know them 'Uncle Bill' and 'Aunt Pat'.

The Butlers then headed back to San Francisco from 1936-1939, spending some time in Los Angeles, Fort Leavenworth Kansas and Fort Belvoir Virginia in his role as U.S. Army Corp Engineer.

Treasure Island (1938-1940)

As Engineer, and still in Service, he directed construction of the Treasure Island landfill, supervised building Treasure Island as Assistant Director of Public Buildings and Parks for the 1939-40 Golden Gate International Exposition and supervised roadwork of nearby Yerba Buena roadway to Treasure Island and the dredging of shipping channels to Sacramento and Stockton. After the fair ended, Treasure Island was sold to the U.S. Navy to become the base of operations for the war in the Pacific Theatre.

Chapter 3:
World War II (1939-1945)

It wasn't until Mr. Hoover was about to leave the White House – in fact did leave the White House – that Adolph Hitler came into power in 1933.

Then World War II began in Europe on September 1, 1939, when Adolph Hitler invaded Poland. Great Britain and France responded by declaring war soon Germany on September 3rd.

The attack at Pearl Harbor December 7, 1941 prompted Franklin Delano Roosevelt (FDR) to declare war against Japan. The next day, Germany declared war on the Unites States. Roosevelt and Churchill agreed to launch the invasion of Europe in the Spring of 1943.

Instead of France, an alternative site to relieve pressure from Soviet Union for a second front and meet Roosevelts demand that U.S. Forces engage Germans as soon as possible, troops were sent to French North Africa.

The United Kingdoms Prime Minister Winston Churchills vision was that by occupying Morocco, Algeria and Tunisia, we would trap Erwin Rommels Africa Korp between Anglo-American forces in the west and British in Egypt.

Erwin Rommel, known as the "the Desert Fox" commanded the German Africa Corps during the North African campaign of World War II. And he was Adolph Hitlers favorite general but would later be implicated in a plot to assassinate Hitler. (He committed suicide in October 1944.)

Roosevelt approved the North Africa Invasion plan in July 1942. Granddaddy landed with the U.S. invasion force in North Africa where he was transferred from the engineers to the infantry in 1943.

Rankings and Promotions

Major (July 1, 1940)

He was a Commanding Officer of the 1st Engineers from July 1940 to June 1942.

Lieutenant Colonel (September 15, 1941)

He was still a Commanding Officer of the 1st Engineers

Army of the United States

Colonel (1942-1944)

He was promoted to Colonel on February 1, 1942. He was General Staff, 1st Infantry Division to December 1942 in the European Theatre of Operations (Mediterranean) to December 1942.

Until February 23, 1942, , he was involved in the African campaign as G-3 in the Advance Headquarters, II Corps, in Tunisia 1943 through February 23, 1943. G-3 is the informal designation for the Deputy Chief of Staff for operations and Plans. He was responsible for training, operations, plans, and force development.

From North Africa to Italy, he was Colonel Commanding Officer of the 168th Infantry Regiment of the 34th Infantry Division in the North Africa and Italian campaigns until January 1944, tasked with commanding the regiment.

North Africa (1943)

In 1943, he was sent to North Africa where he made the transfer from the engineers to the infantry- Eisenhower sent them to replace the tired and badly shaken fighting "Free French" - while German General Erwin Rommel was pushed out of Egypt into Libya and defeated by British Troops and eventually Tunisia where he led the Afrika Korps.

Rommel entered Tunisia in February 1943, attempting to stall the Allies with defensive operations[9]. Most of the German strength was blocking the approach to Tunisia in the northern area and reinforcements were continuing to arrive in Tunisia by air and sea. However, the Allies eventually forced the Axis forces into a pocket along the Tunisian coast and the Germans surrendered in May 1943.

Gafsa, Tunisia

Granddaddy was stationed at the city of Gafsa, an irrigated fruit growing oasis and connected to the Ports, in west-central Tunisia. The city had a rich history of Roman destruction and Trajan rebuilding and then successfully a center of Byzantine, Arab, Amazigh (Berber) and Ottoman rulers.

Excavations at prehistoric sites in the Gafsa area have yielded artefacts and skeletal remains with the Capsian culture; this Mesolithic civilization has been radiocarbon dated to between 10,000 and 6,000 BCE. During the War, Gafsa suffered heavy

---

9 Wikipedia 1/17/25 "Rommel"

bombardment from both the German and Italian side and the Allies. Part of its Kasbah – their ancient fortress.

He was Deputy Chief of Staff II Corps and Commander Allied Task Force in Gafsa, Tunisia, commanding an international force, to February 23, 1943 , leaving the same day as the Axis forces withdrawal northwest of Kasserine Pats and a night before Rommel began the German Nazi withdrawal after getting pounded by vastly superior U.S. air forces and confronted by dominating strength in front. But only after heavy losses. As General Truscott would later say 'the costs in men and material had fallen heavily upon the American troops of the II Corps'.

IN THE WORDS OF GENERAL TRUSCOTT

"American soldiers who survived the bitter months of January and February 1943 in Tunisia will never forget them – or forget Tunisia. For it was during this period in the deserts and mountains of that ancient land, amid the ruins of a long dead Roman civilization, that American forces first crossed swords with veteran German legions and learned of war from them – the hard way. There, American soldiers, suffering from faults in leadership, from their own ignorance, from inferior equipment, reeled in defeat and yet rose to victory."

-General Lucian K. Truscott, Command Missions, A Personal Story by Lucian K. Truscott page 77[1]

Earlier on February 10th, it was determined that the Gafsa force could not be strengthened enough to hold it against any probable enemy force. If necessary, the Gafsa force would be evacuated toward Feriana where a counterattack could be mounted in sufficient strength. In the Advance Headquarters, II Corps, at the Hotel de France in Gafsa, Granddaddy relieved the acting General and in conjunction with the French colonel, directed operations by a mixed American and French command as far as El Guettar. This area was screened to the east and south by security detachments and roving patrols beyond it.

Gafsa was ordered to be evacuated after radio messages were intercepted that Germans were planning a surprise attack on the Tunisian front in far greater strength than anything so far. Plans for offense were scuttled in and we went into defense mode. Gafsa was to be evacuated.

However, General Truscott did not agree based on his own intelligence access; there was nothing to substantiate alarm over the possibility of a German attack. He wanted to hold Gafsa to protect our forward airfields in the southern area for quick victory. His view was that we should destroy Rommel's' army before it escaped into the Tunisian bridgehead. He told all this to General Eisenhower when he visited American troops here on Feb 12th. But by the night of February 14th, the General directed Gafsa to evacuate.

The 168th Infantry was withdrawn and repositioned; there were losses by the 168th Infantry of the 34th Division through the encirclements.

By February 17th, after all the battles around Sidi Bou Zid, the Allies had not only abandoned Gafsa but also Feriana. Expecting in his "Gafsa Operation" that Gafsa would be lightly held, Romells prime endeavor to disperse and destroy the American II Corps in the general vicinity of Gafsa had been accomplished.

On March 6th, Allied Force made a big change to the U.S. II Corps Commander to Major General George S. Patton Jr. whom General Eisenhower selected. He was brought to Tunisia from Morocco, taking command on March 6th, 1943.

The American divisions in II Corps required a certain amount of strengthening and reorganizing too, especially the 34th Division 168th Infantry which lost its commanding officer (Col. Thomas D. Drake) and much of their strength near Sidi Bou Zid. Granddaddy from G-3, II Corps, became its new commander.

While II Corps was engaged in the battles for Gafsa, Maknassy and El Guettar, the 34th Infantry Division was attempting to gain the important gap through the Eastern Dorsal near Fondouk El Aouareb. If the Allies could drive back the enemy out of their mountain defenses successfully, there would be a chance to cut off the enemy's forces in the southern portion of the Tunisian bridgehead.

The March 25th plan was for the 34th Infantry Division to attack as early as possible. The attack at 6 am on March 27th approached the pass from the southwest. The 34th Division's two regiments

38

organized with the somewhat more experienced 168th Infantry commanded by Granddaddy on the right nearer the enemy's principal hill positions and the 135th Infantry on the northwest.

After not encountering any enemy fire, shells were fired at them. Most of the fire fell on the 168th Infantry. American artillery drove off an enemy reconnaissance group of scout cars and two light tanks. The volume of fire intensified; the troops, including the 168th Infantry, headed for somewhat separated destinations, were only partly successful.

While more attacks continued the next morning with three days of small infantry attacks. Further south, elements of the 168th Infantry gained some isolated hills. On the morning of March 31st, a mobile armored force struck an enemy group hiding in the cactus and olive tree groves about 5 miles south of the main battle area, driving them out despite strong enemy fire from adjacent hills and an air attack by German dive bombers. This operation lost two tanks but is thought to have thwarted an enemy attack at the 168th Infantry's southern flank.

Then in April, the 34th Division passed from II Corps to operational control of the British 9 Corps. Offensive operations by II Corp in central and southern Tunisia were now at an end.

Award of the Distinguished Service Cross

*Colonel Butler has continually exposed himself to enemy fire; without regard to his own personal welfare, in order to inspire the members of his command. His presence in the front lines and his close contact with the advance elements of his command exemplify his **fearlessness, aggressiveness and complete devotion to duty.***

Italy

Grandaddy was in Italy by late 1943.

As Colonel, Infantry and Commanding Officer, on January 20, 1944, Granddaddy received the Award of Distinguished Service Cross from the Headquarters Fifth Army for 'extraordinary heroism in action' in Italy in late 1943. He had led his command to each succeeding objective, displaying 'aggressive and inspirational leadership of the highest order.

Furthermore, he was commended for coming forward and accompanying his troops on their mission, encouraging them to greater efforts when the Battalion of his Regiment was ordered to make a crucial attack in Italy. Again, in October, when one of his battalions was halted by enemy fire, he personally rallied the officers and men, within full view of the enemy and under continuous small arms fire, organizing a successful resumption of the attack.

To quote the Award of Distinguished Service Cross language itself 'Colonel Butler has continually exposed himself to enemy fire; without regard to his own personal welfare, in order to inspire the members of his command. His presence in the front lines and his close contact with the advance elements of his command exemplify his **fearlessness, aggressiveness and complete devotion to duty.**

Brigadier General (1944-1948)

He was then promoted to Brigadier General in January of 1944, as they began the campaign in Italy and later the invasion of Southern France, where most importantly, as Brigadier General in VI Corps, he led the Butler Task Force brigade into the Battle of Montelimar.

From February 1944 to March 1944, he was in Italy as Assistant Division Commander, 34th Infantry Division.

From March 1944 to September 1944, he was in the Italy campaign and then onto the invasion of southern France for Operation Dragoon (ANVIL) with the VI Corps as Assistant to Commander VI Corps to General Lucien Truscott. Truscott then assigned him to be Commander of Task Force Butler, an ad hoc group he had formed initially for some unplanned reconnaissance, but would end up busting through the German lines, cutting off the retreating German Nineteenth Army in Southern France, liberating towns as they went (More on that later).

He took his men 240 miles right up the Rhone Valley. It's been said to be **one of the greatest feats of World War II,** finishing up his most triumphant war operation of his career, commanding Task Force Butler in southern France. According to his Commander General Truscott, without Granddaddy's' Task Force speed of execution and heroic pursuit of the enemy, 'we would not have been able to gain the rear of the German XIX Army at Montelimar, which considerably hindered the Germans escape, pushing back their lines of defense.

Then from September 1944 to January 1945, in southern France, he continued as Assistant Division Commander to the 45th Division for the battles around Montelimar in Loriol sur Drome during Operation Dragoon, an area remembered for its stench from the hundreds of dead horses and dead bodies littering the road.

Italy

Let's start by talking about the campaign in Italy.

After the great victory in North Africa in 1943 by our Allied land forces, the British, especially Winston Churchill felt the need to continue the momentum of attack by engaging the Germans as quickly as possible and distract from France and Russia – with an invasion across the English Channel and a drive on Berlin and that Italy was the country to best do that. The Americans wanted to attack direct- anything else would be a side show - and had a serious strategic difference of opinion for many reasons, especially the peculiar tactical difficulty of the terrain. The widely held theory though was that the German armies could not effectively fight in Italy.

However, that was wishful thinking.

Anzio (Jan 1944- Feb 1944)

'Few geographical names relating to military operation in World War II became known to more people than the name "Anzio", and few operations in World War II have occasioned more controversy'. [10]

They were all aware that this Italian campaign was only secondary to the cross-channel Normandy invasion which was to take place in the Spring and the Anzio beach landing would put ashore 50,000 men and 5,000 vehicles with only seven days

---

10 Truscott?

ammunition and supplies on January 24, 1944. They weren't even sure there would be landing craft available.

The beachhead assault at Anzio was to be launched in January 1944, despite awful weather, to take advantage of a small window of time when there was sufficient landing craft available for an invasion in the Mediterranean before it was needed for the Normandy invasion.

It would turn out to be a long and costly battle. Americas' strategic reluctance to throw its full weight into Italy and the Italian geography left troops undersupplied and understaffed.

The new battle would instead begin on January 24th against strong wind gales, rough seas, increasing German counter-strength and a renascent Nazi Luftwaffe which had come out of hiding to deliver some sharp blows, including the destruction of a hospital ship full with the wounded and a destroyer sunk by dropped bombs from enemy planes on that day at dusk.

Troops sought shelter in caves, hollowed from canal banks, in tanks, trucks, and other vehicles. A few stone farmhouses in forward areas remained standing for housing command posts and aid stations where frontline company men could occasionally get a hot meal and dry out their clothing. As commander, Granddaddy probably used caravans and trailers as homes and offices.

Only 33 miles south of Rome, this is where Granddaddy first worked with General Lucian K. Truscott. They trusted each other and worked well together. Truscott had a high opinion

of him. He later wrote about Granddaddy "He had been my assistant corps Commander since Anzio. He was thoroughly familiar with all my views and he was one of the most fearless men I ever met".

The time spent in Anzio with him would set the stage for him later selecting him to lead an ad hoc group of men into enemy lines, marching towards Montelimar in southern France while Operation Dragoon in Normandy was getting under way. It was an important, perilous job that he would tap him to command in August later that year with only weeks of preparation. It would come to be known as Task Force Butler (TFB).

To give you an idea as to the man who was his commander, here is a little about General Truscott...

General Lucian K. Truscott

Truscott, a former schoolteacher from Texas, was a quiet, competent, and courageous officer with great battle experience through North Africa, Sicily, and Italy, he inspired confidence in all whom he came in contact[11].

> **"Wars aren't won by gentlemen. They're won by men who can be first-class sons of bitches when they have to be. It's as simple as that. No son of a bitch, no commander."**
>
> *- General Lucian K. Truscott, Jr.*
> *Command Missions,*
> *A personal story*
> *1954.*

"The general would transform the members of the 3rd Infantry Division, one of the army's oldest, in his crucible so that they could meet the challenges ahead. He was confident that the better he trained each soldier, the more likely it was that man would one day make it home.[12] One of his Commanders in World War II in North Africa and the Mediterranean theatre, General Truscott summed up soldiers' first reaction to the battlefield as well as anyone by saying in his memoirs[13] that

"While we can approximate the physical conditions of battle including the extreme of fatigue, discomfort, and sound effects, we cannot create in peace time all of the psychological conditions and tensions that result from the uncertainty, loneliness, and horror incident to war. "

---

11 General Mark W. Clark, Calculated Risk, pp 244-245
12 Ferguson 2015 p. 145
13 Command Missions, Truscott, In Afterthoughts

46

In the beginning of February at Anzio, he said *"The successful commander must display a spirit of confidence regardless of the dark outlook in any grim situation, and he must be positive and stern in the application of measures which will impress this confidence upon his command"*.

Truscott believed in a high level of training. *His principal objectives were to attain the highest possible speed-marching and physical standards and to develop initiative and leadership among officers and non-commissioned officers. As men reached increasingly difficult standards; self-confidence grew.* Weeding out the weak developed pride amongst those who could do the work. In promoting men:

1) Insisted that battle was a simple business when conducted by common sense methods and by soldiers who were physically fit and knew how to use their weapons;

2) They were all capable of working together in the field as a team;

3) Must be disciplined to withstand hardship and danger in attaining the objective;

4) Never permit any officer to be punished for any mistake when he was acting on his own initiative but did insist commanders deal harshly with failure to act boldly when the situation required it.

Truscott had a big rugged individual personality; In Africa, he wore a russet or red leather jacket. He adopted this as a personal uniform with a shiny lacquered helmet so that every soldier in the Division could recognize him from afar. In Sicily, his allergies from the choking dust and exhaust fumes and trucks brought tears streaming from his eyes while they marched, causing sneezing and coughing. So he took his pocket handkerchief which was a cloth map of Sicily and tied around his neck as a scarf, drawing it up over his face like a mask, like a cowboy bandana. As days passed, he noticed more and more men wearing similar scarves to protect their faces and necks and shirt collars from sweat and dirt. It enhanced esprit, amusement as well as filled a practical need. His scarf was white so others had to select some other color but each unit would select a distinctive one. Nothing formal – all done by word of mouth, becoming soon a recognized part of the uniform. Soon salvaged parachutes and captured silk were at a premium.

He was known for his talented Chinese cooks and waiters that went everywhere with him, always ready to prepare and serve cocktails and a good meal.

Two of his non-negotiable rules were 1) Wear a helmet at all times, and 2) No vehicle would carry more than its authorized passenger load i.e. jeeps 4 persons.

Granddaddys nephew Lewis would say in an interview later that Granddaddy never shared stories after the War, but that he had an orderly while in Italy. His name was Scalese; he was this Italian guy from Brooklyn who didn't want to get shot in the war, so he made himself into an orderly to a general - which was Granddaddy. And after the war, Scalese would spend some time with Lewis. He'd tell Lewis stories about Granddaddy, including when they were pinned down at Anzio beachhead for four months. And Scalese said it was terrible. He said the Germans were shelling every night. And then apparently, this one time, Scalese found a cache of booze somewhere in somebody's basement in Anzio. And he said, 'That night, we brought the booze up and we all sat on the roof and drank.' Including Granddaddy. And when they finally broke out from Anzio, he had been put in charge of the artillery barrage that softened up the German lines so we could break through.

Again, more on that later....

Figure 5
http://findagrave.com//memorial/47303105/frederic-bates-butler

Figure 6 Wikipedia 8/24

Cassino (Jan 17ᵗʰ 1944 – June 4ᵗʰ 1944)

Before the War, halfway between Naples and Rome, Cassino was a typical Italian country town of 25,000 population. Noisy, cheerful, busy and in the summer hot and dusty; It had history going back to fourth century B.C.

Its special claim to fame rests on the great mountain which rears up behind the town and bears its name. In the 6ᵗʰ century, Mount Cassino was founded by the monk Benedict, founding the Benedict Order and set in motion one of the great civilizing movements of history.

The Abbey of Mount Cassino was founded in A.D 529 by St. Benedict. On a former site of a temple for Apollo– not an especially beautiful massive building that was impressive but the beauty of the setting as a whole. The Benedictine Monastery at Cassino is a sacred site of Christianity.

A natural fortress sanctuary, it suffered four destructions – two by opposing forces the Lombars in 581 and the Saracens in 883, and one by earthquake (1349)

In 1944, there were no trees on the slopes of Monte Cassino. Spring was late. As guardian of the road to Rome, it once again lied in the path of a war. U.S. military forces had to go through Cassino to get to Rome.

Rome was a symbol. The prize. But the Army must break thru Cassino to get there.

---

14 Calculated Risk by Clark Page 311

The battle of Cassino would become the battle for Rome, ending June 4th, 1944 when 5th Army entered Rome. Two days after the fall of Rome the Allies invaded Normandy and the Italian campaign took a back seat to France. Cassino was the climatic show of strength fought exhaustively to the finish when Germany did not consider the war yet lost.

One Gustov Line

From January 24th until Feb 11th, both armies had been at a standstill. A dozen miles of rugged mountain terrain and stubbornly defending enemy lay between our battle-worn and depleted divisions and the line of the Gagliano and Rapido Rivers – the Gustav Line which the Germans were already fortifying.

On the northward advance up the Italian peninsula to Rome, the U.S. Army would need to bypass the Gustuv Line that was blocked by the Germans; it was hinged on Mt. Cassino.

Few battles WWII battles – or of any war – compare to the epic grandeur and classic tragedy of Cassino. There was a brooding presence from Mount Cassino itself that gave the battlefield an almost theatrical quality. The Battle of Rapido River was the bloodiest battle of the Italian campaign; It was a suicide mission to try to cross an unfordable, swiftly flowing River under heavy enemy fire. Yet it was a deliberate strategy to draw the Germans there in order to safeguard our landing of 50,000 men at Anzio.

First, the British soldiers ferried themselves across the Garigliano and then the Americans slogged across the flooded Rapido River valley after the Germans had blasted the dam, turning already soggy terrain around Cassino into a quagmire that swallowed men and vehicles, filled with unseen mines and boobytraps, and unknowingly starting the battle of Cassino. They were merely continuing, after a few days pause, a painful advance through mud, mountain and river with Germans fighting from their prepared positions.

The dam blown apart by the enemy produced the greatest flooding effect in the section of the valley they must cross. On the far side of the river, the Allied forces were met with enemy fire, raining down artillery and mortar fire, wire, and extensive minefields, and a great wall of mountains rising, almost vertically, immediately behind the river and running southwards in a tight mass to Mount Cassino a mile and half to their left. They would have to cross two miles of marsh - wading an icy river or floating on inflatable rafts - and then attack the mountains head-on, while the comfortably entrenched enemy, watching them all the way across from multiple locations, picking the men off as they pleased. It was a slaughter.

Two days after the failed Rapido River crossing and landing at Anzio, the 34th joined the fight to grab Cassino from the North. Granddaddy was the deputy commander of the 34th division during the first attack on Cassino.

The first battle of Cassino was not a prepared offensive against the Gustav line, but a hurried resumption of a weary advance that had battered its way to a standstill. Exhausted by weeks of fighting, severe casualties and appalling weather conditions, troops badly in need of a break were in effect told to keep going. The plan looked coherent on paper but the first assault on one of the most powerful defensive systems of the war was hastily put together without any proper preparation.

Even though he was one of the local commanders, this was not Granddaddy's fault. It was entirely due to the deadline imposed by the Anzio landing, ill-timed shipping schedules and landing craft shortages.

Day after day, night after night, Americans clung miserably to their bare slopes and tried to inch forward. Slopes were littered with dead. Heavy rain fell all day. When they were finally relieved by British and Indian soldiers, the few who had held on to the last were too numb with cold and exhaustion to move. The soldiers still manned their positions, but many could not move without aid. Carried out on stretchers, some were then killed on their stretchers by shellfire on the long, tortuous way down to safety.

When New Zealand and Indian troops moved in to relieve them, the men were too cold and exhausted to move, taken away on stretchers[15] . It was one of the final cruelties of this battle that some of them, having survived so much, were killed on their stretchers on the long, tortuous way down to safety.'

Battle casualties: 7000 killed, 36000 wounded and MIA. 44,000 received hospital care for sickness and injury.

---

15 Cassino Page 87

"The performance of the 34th Division at Cassino must rank with the finest feats of arms carried out by any soldiers during the war'.
Cassino Fred Majdalny

The Abbey of Mount Cassino

As assistant division commander of the 34th division during the attack on Cassino, Granddaddy made the first attacks on the Monastery Feature and made some noticeable progress breaking through the German battlefront as recognized by General Clark who said *'The 36th Divisions efforts to outflank Cassino from the south at the Rapido River had been unsuccessful, but the 34th division, later trying a flanking attack north of town, made a small but important breach in the enemy line'*[16].

The reluctant decision to also bomb the historically significant and ancient holy Benedictine Abbey was very controversial but was ultimately made.

It was a shame. On February 15, 1944 allied bombers dropped 1,400 tonnes (1543.236 U.S. tons) of high explosives, causing widespread damage, allowing for the German forces occupying the area to establish defensive positions amid the ruins.

By doing so, one of the art treasures of the world was destroyed along with 300-400 civilian women and children taking shelter there. It was a rushed decision; evacuation leaflets were dropped

---

16 Clarke page 313

but none fell inside the abbey walls. Altogether tons of bombs were dropped yet there was no evidence of any German occupation nor was it ever confirmed.

It was a long drawn out agonizing battle of heroic deadlock with gallantry on both sides during a long cold and wet winter. The soldiers endured horrible natural terrain and weather difficulties, ultimately resulting in 55,000 Allied casualties.

'The Battle of Cassino was the most grueling, the most harrowing, and in one aspect perhaps the most tragic, of any phase of the war in Italy.'

U.S. Army General Mark. W. Clark (Calculated Risk page 311).

Granddaddy had recommended against it. At the U.S. Corps handing over to 2nd New Zealand Corps conference, he expressed his concern over the necessity of the attack, saying ***"I don't know but I don't believe the enemy is in the convent. All the fire has been from the slopes of the hill below the wall"[17]***

The Abbey of Monte Cassino was believed to be part of the German defensive system. As deputy commander of the 34th Division, Granddaddy was one of three that had command in the sector. Everyone agreed it was unnecessary and that it would only

---

17 Cassino Majdalany 1957 page 140

fail to assist the attacking troops but also make our job much more difficult by letting the Germans feel perfectly free to use the ruins of the buildings as defensive positions. There were intelligence reports that there were as many as 2000 refugees in the Monastery but no reports of any actual fire coming from the buildings. Even General Clark, did not think the buildings should be bombed since no military necessity exists for the destruction of the Monastery.

The bombing was initially delayed because of bad weather with a total of 255 Allied bombers participating in the attack, dropping tons of explosives. Then it is was shelled by our artillery.

General Mark W. Clark[18]

[1]Clark, a longtime friend of Dwight Eisenhower, was one of the essential quartet of American leaders who achieved victory in Europe along with Dwight D. Eisenhower, George S. Patton, Omar N. Bradley and Mark Clark. He was 47 years old at Cassino, the youngest four-star general in the U.S. Army during the War. At 6'2", Clark was always in danger of being concussed in the cramped confines of submarines.

General Clark would later say, "*Not only was the bombing of the Abbey an unnecessary psychological mistake in the propaganda*

---

18 Clark was one of the essential quartet of American leaders who achieved victory in Europe along with Dwight D. Eisenhower, George S. Patton, Omar N. Bradley and MARK CLARK. He was 47 years old at Cassino, the youngest four-star general in the U.S. Army during the War. At 6'2", Clark was always in danger of being concussed in the cramped confines of submarines.

field, but it was a tactical military mistake of the first magnitude"

The General, a key figure in WWII, was splitting his time between commanding both Anzio and Cassino troops. He did not recommend the bombing either but when General Freberg asked for the bombing 'tomorrow', Clark wasn't available for an hour and his opinion was dismissed. When he weighed in, he said 'the bombing is not a military necessity.'

Clark would say in his memoirs[19] that *'The Battle of Cassino was the most grueling, the most harrowing, and in one aspect perhaps the most tragic, of any phase of the war in Italy. When I think back on weeks and finally months of searing struggle, the biting cold, the torrents of rain and snow, the lakes of mud that sucked down machines and men, and most of all, the deeply dug fortifications in which the Germans waited for us in the hills, it seems to me that no soldiers in history were ever given a more difficult assignment than the Fifth Army in that winter of 1944. And I am certain that no men in combat ever fought more gallantly against such incredible odds.'*

General Clark said that the bombing of the Abbey was a mistake[20]. He said at the time *'there was no evidence that the Germans were using the Abbey for military purposes. And after the war, confirmed that there is irrefutable evidence that no*

____

19 Calculated Risk, Mark Clark, page 311
20 Calculate Risk, Mark W. Clark See back cover

Figure 7 Cassino Monastery before the bombing

Figure 9 Lt. General Mark Clark (the youngest four star general in the US Army during WWII) pins an insignia on Granddaddy in the 34th infantry.

General Truscott would later express his frustration over Anzio and Cassino saying Anzio was a massacre at the beachhead two months after our landing caught the Germans by surprise, leaving living accommodations extremely primitive. And out of 767 highly-trained Rangers sent to Cistern only 6 made their way back to friendly lines after getting surrounded by the Germans. Wiped out. Cassino was poorly and hastily executed due to the time and supply constraints imposed by Anzio.

Following Anzio, Truscott continued fighting up the Italian boot, helping in the final Battle of Monte Cassino and the subsequent capture of Rome, just two days before the Normandy landings. However, his command was then withdrawn to begin preparations for Operation Dragoon, another amphibious assault on southern France. The American focus was shifting from Italy to Southern France.

Based on historical significance and magnitude, the Normandy invasion of France would not only overshadow the success of capturing Rome in Italy but eclipse all battles of World War I and II and every clash of arms in the history of peoples and nations.

Southern France (Aug 15 –Sept 14, 1944)

So then Granddaddy moved up to the French Riviera for the second Allied invasion (the first was two months earlier at Normandy) along the southern French Coast and was put in charge by General Truscott of something called Butler's Task Force, driving up over 200 miles from the South of France to Berlin during Operation Dragoon.

"It was a helluva headache, but it was a helluva lot of fun", he told war correspondents later. "The Germans never knew where we were or what we were".

In His Own Words

"It was a helluva headache, but it was a helluva lot of fun. The Germans never knew where we were or what we were."

Frederick Butler, talking about his time in France.
Quoted in obituary 6.24.87

Operation Dragoon (August 1 -30, 1944)

Originally, Anvil/Dragoon was intended to be a simultaneous landing with Operation Overlord in Normandy designed to stretch German defenses thin between the two fronts. But the delays in breaking out from the Italian Anzio beachhead coupled with shortages of landing craft forced the cancellation. With the fall of Rome on June 4th and naval forces allocated to Normandy became available again, General Truscott's plan was reactivated in mid-July.

Sandwiched between allied efforts in Northern France and Italy, Dragoon would be one of the most successful but controversial campaigns of WWII.

Originally code-named ANVIL, Operation Dragoon marked the second allied invasion of southern France in the late summer of

'44. Intended to support the blow of the Normandy beach landings two months earlier,

Operation Dragoon seemed almost like an afterthought to the main Allied offensive in northern Europe, yet its success, together with the capture of the great southern ports of Toulon and Marseilles and the subsequent drive north up the Rhone valley to Lyon and Dijon, were ultimately to provide the critical support necessary to the Normandy-based armies finally moving east toward the German border.

'The landing and subsequent advance up the Rhone River Valley to link up with troops breaking out from Normandy beachhead proved to be one of the most significant, and underrated, strategic campaigns of the entire war.'[21]

Operation Dragoon has been overshadowed by the later efforts to liberate Rome and Paris the same summer. However, it clearly and undoubtedly played a major role in ensuring the eventual Allied War victory, remaining a model of campaign planning and execution for military professionals today.

On August 13th, 1944, in the Port of Naples after coordinating the preparations for the second French beach head invasion, Winston Churchill stepped into a speedboat to salute the fleet heading off

---

21 Operation Dragoon:Invasion of Southern France" Chris Rein PHD, Article WWII The National WWII Museum New Orleans

for the invasion. The heat was most oppressive. The ventilating system was broken on Truscott's ship. There were 1001 ships sailing to commence the attack on the French Riviera shores.

On August 15th, 1944, the sun came up on a clear Mediterranean morning before any of the early Autumn thunderstorms. At 8 am, an allied army force launched a set of amphibious landings by three US infantry divisions followed by four French divisions along the Mediterranean coast of Southern France. The Battle began along a 25 mile strip of shoreline east of Toulon.

Allied landing craft put ashore 66,000 soldiers and 6,500 tactical vehicles along a 30-mile stretch of the French Riviera between Toulon and Cannes. Another 9,000 paratroopers and glider troops were dropped from planes 12 miles inland near the town of Le Muy.

The Allied troops stormed ashore against light and disorganized German resistance, opening a new front on continental Europe. Adolph Hitler called August 15th the "worst day of my life".

The main landings were preceded by nighttime paratroop drops and commando beach landings, enabling the Allies to liberate most of Southern France in just four weeks while shattering German defenses in combat around the beachhead and inflicting heavy casualties on the German forces. 12,129 German prisoners; 183 Allied casualties. The ports of Marseilles and Toulon were soon in operation again.

However, many Germans escaped. To catch them, they would need to be trapped between the Italian and Swiss borders, marked by Maritime and High Alps to the East; the Rhone River on the West.

If an air force could destroy the Rivers bridges, German armies would be isolated from each other on either side of the River. Beyond the River, they could only escape northward by roads. The vital point on this route was several miles north of Montelimer, the small French city on the east bank of the Rhone River, a critical chokepoint for the German evacuation route.

The main ground force for the operation was the United States Seventh Army commanded by Alexander Patch. The U.S. Army's VI Corps, commanded by Major General Lucian Truscott, would carry out the initial landing and be followed by the French Army B.

Truscott, selected by General Clark, had become the new VI Corps commander because of all the division commanders available to General Clark in the Anzio bridgehead who were familiar with the situation, he was said to be the most outstanding.

More about General Truscott

In France in 1944, Granddaddy was a Brigadier General and serving as General Lucien Truscott's assistant Corps Commander. It was an honor; Few generals achieved the reputation won by Lucien Truscott during his time in the U.S. Army during World War II. The future President General

Eisenhower said that Truscott was second only to the legendary General Patton as a battlefield commander. He was tough, determined and cool under fire.

He had enrolled at the First Officers Training Camp, entering Army as a cavalry officer but saw no overseas service during WWI. From 1919-1925, he commanded a cavalry troop stationed along Mexican border. Then back to Cavalry school for 6 years as a student & 4 years as an instructor. He commanded another troop at Fort Myer Virginia 1931-1934. From 1934-36, he was a member of the last 2-year class Command and General Staff School at Fort Leavenworth Texas and another 4 years there as instructor. Between 1940-1952, he spent six months in an armor regiment in the 1st Armored Division as General Staff of IX Army Corps (9 mos.), and then six months commanding the 7th Cavalry Regiment in the 1st Cavalry Division (all his early Army experience was with horses not tanks) and then left for his first wartime mission in May 1942 to London with Letter of Instructions from Major General Dwight D. Eisenhower. All these were important steps in his military education and development as a battle leader.

'Most British generals who came in contact with him *'rated Truscott the best American General in Italy'*. Blunt, forthright practical soldier with no time for frills. Always outspoken[22].

In his memoirs. Truscott observed that the men, entering battle for the first time, were keyed to high pitch of nervous tension.

---

22 Cassino page 73 1942-1947

It had never occurred to him that naval gunfire passing over the heads of an infantry battalion could cause such panic that the battalion would take to its heels and disperse so that it would take almost two days to collect the stragglers. Yet no shell fell within a thousand yards of the battalion, and no enemy was firing upon it. He surmised that there were two causes for this. 1) the battalion was not familiar with the sound of naval gunfire passing overhead, having just landed on a strange and hostile shore, advancing in darkness on a dangerous mission was nerve racking, breaking completely under a new and terrifying sound. And 2) Training had neglected to familiarize the men to the sounds of battle and failed to instill the rigorous discipline and control to prevent these panics.

In General Truscotts Own Words
"One must actually experience the hardships of war to understand the awful strain, both mental and physical, which battle imposes upon men, the dreadful fatigue and fear which destroys the will and poisons every fiber. And I had observed a tendency on the part of the commanders and comrades to sympathize and pity. I felt little of these sentiments during battle, and moreover felt we could not permit them to deflect men from their duty. We could not give way to weariness for that would only give the enemy an advantage. We could not allow able-bodied men to take care of wounded or sick comrades until the battle was won. This drive is an important function of command"

-Gen Lucian Truscott
Command Missions, A Personal Story, 1954

He also noticed too many strong and brave men were easily surrendering to French opponents while fighting in North Africa but training had actually taught them to surrender when they were caught at a disadvantage.

"Most officers and men lacked confidence in themselves and were hesitant and uncertain in battle. They were inclined to wait for a superior to tell them what to do. Even though the action may have been perfectly obvious or even specified in orders, they were reluctant to assume responsibility. Yet again, the men were not wholly to blame since in training no junior officer could deviate from the text or regulations or orders without risking harsh criticism.", he observed later in his memoirs.

Also, later writing that *"One must actually experience the hardships of war to understand the awful strain, both mental and physical, which battle imposes upon men, the dreadful fatigue and fear which destroys the will and poisons every fiber. And I had observed a tendency on the part of the commanders and comrades to sympathize and pity. I felt little of these sentiments during battle, and moreover felt we could not permit them to deflect men from their duty. We could not give way to weariness for that would only give the enemy an advantage. We could not allow able-bodied men to take care of wounded or sick comrades until the battle was won. This drive is an important function of command".*[23]

---

23 Truscott

Figure 10 General Lucien Truscott wikipedia

Truscott interestingly also noted later in his memoirs that there was a culture challenge between the Americans and the Brits. The British considered Americans to be loud, boastful, and inexperienced.

The British considered battle as something of a game and to adopt a sporting attitude toward the German enemy even in defeat. American soldiers had none of this attitude. Americans play games to win; they fight battles in the same spirit. Our soldiers knew when they had taken a licking but they did not like it. Defeat did not depress them, nor affect their natural conceit; they only felt a burning anger. "Wherever I went, reequipping armored units, officers and men said to me: 'Give us tanks and equipment. We can lick these Germans. We know how to do it now".

Chapter 4:
Task Force Butler
(August 1 – 30, 1944)

Some say it was August 1st that the idea of forming a fast-moving, provisional armored, exploration group first came to General Truscott in his Naples headquarters while planning to land three American divisions along the French Riviera as part of Operation Dragoon with largely foot-mobile troops. (The 3rd, 36th and 45th Infantry.). But in fact, it was back in July, Truscott decided to form a small, mobile striking force under his asst. corps commander in case the combat command of the French Armored Division (a floating reserve) would be taken from him and returned to the French control shortly after landing in Southern France, leaving him without a reconnaissance unit.

So as a back-up plan, he picked Granddaddy, a 47-year old career soldier, to organize a Provisional Armored Group from elements of the Corps, handing him enormous responsibility. Turning toward him, Truscott said, 'And if there is such a force, I want you to command it.' "[24] Truscott trusted Granddaddy. He had been the Generals assistant Corps Commander since Anzio and was thoroughly familiar with all his views.

---

24 Warfare History Network 'Operation Dragoon: The Allied Invasion of France in the South" April 2020

As his assistant and an experienced officer and combat leader, Truscott entrusted Granddaddy to be the first and only member of his Task Force.

Granddaddy then solely selected his staff who then had to locate vehicles and equipment as none were currently available. Many of the men he chose had worked with him at Anzio during combat operations and in battle. He said later they 'were my all-stars – but that does not guarantee a winning team'.

In His Own Words

"It is appreciated readily that best results are obtained when units have been trained together in the tactical entity in which they are to fight. Any sportsman realized that a team of all stars thrown together for the first time is far from an effective game-winning aggregation.

Brigadier General Frederick B. Butler, 1948

"Time was short. My first step was to select a staff from amongst assistants in the various Corps staff sections. Next, a provisional troop list was prepared. Then as the staff was assembled, various studies were assigned-detailed maps reconnaissance of routes, terrain appreciation, air ground cooperation, Maquis Liaison, and most pressing of all, a communications plan".

Truscott believed in an offensive battle; the object is to destroy the enemy, seeking to attack the enemy in flank and rear where he is most vulnerable as he had proven in Africa, Sicily and Italy,

74

He had trained his men for superhuman efforts and had driven them to the limits of human endurance in order to attain it. But the enemy was just as mobile which permitted them to escape before they could close trap. Also, the forces which he had placed in the enemy's rear had not been strong enough to achieve the desired results as seen in the landings on the north coast of Sicily and at Anzio.

The German orders were to keep the escape route open at all costs. Truscott dreamt of the battle in which he could trap the enemy without any avenues or means of escape, assuring the enemies destruction.

So Granddaddy and his staff prepared a plan while in Naples for an advance northwest to the Durance River and then north toward Grenoble or west to seize high ground north of Montelimar to block a German withdrawal through the Montelimar Gap east of the Rhone.

As Granddaddy said, it was back in July that General Truscott had decided to form a small mobile striking force under him soon after the initial beach landings and chose him to lead it.

Forming the new, multi-unit, Task Force was a new untested fighting concept. The idea was only a couple of weeks old. Introducing combat command, customizing combined arms organizations that would be task organized, assembling staff and equipment quickly to execute a new strategy all while changing to meet needs of each mission.

Granddaddy drew primarily from the 36th Division, including a motorized battalion from the 141st Infantry, two medium tank companies, a tank destroyer, a light cavalry squadron, and a self-propelled artillery battalion. Encouraged by Truscott, a Cavalry man, a principal component of the Force was the 117th Cavalry Reconnaissance Squadron, VI Corps, known as an aggressive, well-armed and highly mobile combat team with an especially robust radio network.

After subsequent conferences, Granddaddy's mission had narrowed to a single possibility. He was to proceed to Sisteron and from there, be prepared to continue north to seize Grenoble or to turn west and seize the high ground north of Montelimar. Division commanders were briefed and the whole plan was approved by Lieutenant General Alexander M. Patch, Commanding General, Seventh Army.

Then late in the afternoon of August 16th, Truscott ordered the Task Force to begin executing the plan on the following day.

On August 17th, Truscott sent only Granddaddy's' light armored force, equal to a combat command of a U.S. armored division, to secure the vital artery, under Granddaddy's' command, designating them collectively as "Task Force Butler".

76

Penetrating more than 125 miles from the beachhead in just a few days (190 miles within 4 days), their bold and aggressive actions forced the surrender of the entire garrison of 1500 enemy soldiers with its commanding officers in the Town of Gap. They opened the heaviest fighting of Operation Dragoon, as over the next week, German forces, including the fierce 11th Panzer, broken through several of our weak roadblocks and '**at one point threatened to surround us and cut off my entire command!**' he would write later.

With the promised – but - late arrival of the 36th Infantry division from the coast, they were finally able to close the corridor with the liberation of Montelimar on August 29th.

The Maquis

Granddaddy and his men were aided significantly by the French Resistance (the Maquis). They were a most notable motley faction of rural guerrilla bands of French and Belgium Resistance fighters, fighting Nazi occupation and were mostly young, working-class men who had escaped into the mountains and woods to avoid capture, torture, death and deportation to German concentration camps. As Task Force commander, Granddaddy was in touch with the Maquis and they eagerly requested his support for German detachments. The Germans seemed to fear this rag tag group of these French Resistance fighters, specifically the guerrilla bands of fighters in rural areas, revolutionaries and would often surrender to the Americans just to avoid a confrontation with them.

Granddaddy wrote *"The German dread of the Maquis came to the surface continuously during our race into the interior. Really, some of our adventurous young officers became quite persuasive salesmen. Many and many a garrison was taken after a few shots—an American advanced under a white flag and a parley[25]. If the German commander could be convinced that he and his force would become American prisoners, and not be turned over to the French, surrender usually was accomplished forthwith."*

I digress. Lets start again.

Once again going back to July, soon after the initial beach landings, as Truscott studied the terrain of eastern France and the many possible outcomes of various strategies, he came up with this new maneuver to form a small, mobile striking force to surround the enemy and he put Granddaddy, his Assistant Corps Commander in charge. Frederic B. Butler. It was to be called Task Force Butler. This Force was then drawn primarily from the 36th division with an inexperienced commander General Dahlquist.

---

25 Def: to speak with another. Specifically, to discuss terms with an enemy. 'Negotiate' without being attacked until the parley is complete (based on Code of Pirates)

Task Force Butler was only a small group of men, heading just 100 miles inland, dependent on already very-strained supply lines stretching back to the coast. They really did not have the combat power to overwhelm the desperate, hard-fighting Germans. But they bravely pushed back from the valley itself, and with some help from the Maquis, set up on the surrounding ridges, inflicting fearful casualties on the dominating Germans.

According to Truscott's later recollections of Granddaddy's operation, ***'His orders were to lead to one of the most gallant exploits of the entire war.'*** While no one in Army Headquarters had anything to do with the organization of Granddaddy's' Task Force, the mission was invariably approved by Truscott's boss (General Alexander "Sandy" Patch). [26]

He had been approved for the enormous task based on that he had been assured by Truscott that Granddaddy to be trusted and that he was 'one of the most fearless men he ever met'.

So on August 1st, Granddaddy formed his staff at once and assisted by the Corps staff, completed the following 3 organizational plans for three lines of actions:

1) An advance to the Durance River in the vicinity of St. Paul to seize crossings there and to the west;

---

26 Historical Note: Sandy Patch and Lucien Truscott were the only 2 U.S. Army officers on active duty during World War II to command a division, corps, and field army.

2) An advance to the Durance River at Manosque to seize crossings in that area; and

3) An advance to the north toward Grenoble to block roads east of the Rhone in the vicinity of Montelimar

For the next four days, Granddaddy finished all facets of organization and every element included as well as notifying the divisions that would be reassigned. They had detailed reconnaissance maps, an understanding of the geography, coordinations with air support and the Maquis detailed map reconnaissance of routes, and most important of all, a short-range communication plan.

The Task Force had a full cavalry squadron (117th) equipped with jeeps and M8 armored cars and reliable FM transceivers. Still unsolved, however, was the issue of long-range communications. They would be hundreds of miles from Truscott's headquarters well beyond the range of any radio in inventory. This shortfall later nearly doomed the operation at a most critical time.

Meanwhile, the vital area lay between the Italian and Swiss borders with the Maritime and High Alps on the east and the broad deep Rhone River on the west. The River had unusually swift currents flowing from the glaciers and lakes of the Swiss Alps. If the Air Force could destroy all the bridges, the Task Force could trap and isolate the German forces on either side of the River.

If they could break through the German coast defenses quickly, the Germans would probably concentrate to oppose them from driving west. If the Task Force could move toward Sisteron and

Grenoble and seize the high ground north of Montelimar, they might be able to block the Germans escape at that time. So the high ground immediately north of Montelimar became a vital factor to block any German retreat up the west bank of the Rhone. But as of then, there was no Army plan or maps drawn for this scenario even though this would be mostly a big win if it occurred. Truscott could never even obtain any assurance from his superior (General Patch) that the French Armored Combat Command would be available to him, if this desirable situation occurred.

This Task Force, drawn primarily from the 36th division with commander General Dalquist, included a motorized battalion from the 141st infantry, two medium tank companies, a tank destroyer company, a light cavalry squadron, and a self-propelled artillery battalion.

They were facing multiple challenges, knowingly handicapping their efforts. For example, they were to strike deep into enemy territory with supply shortages, insecure long-range lines of communication, while also securing large numbers of prisoners deep behind enemy lines and the loss of communications with higher headquarters.

This quickly assembled, ad hoc group of men (and equipment) - with no history of training together and with no training together, no planning, no rehearsals – is now known as the Task Force Butler.

Task forces were common in the U.S. Army during WWII. But unlike other past task forces that were built for a particular mission, Task Force Butler had no pre-existing command structure. Its staff officers had been pulled from assistant staff offices. The Task Force headquarters had no equipment assigned to it. And just one unit.

There were not many tanks available – most equipment was already assigned to other efforts - so they were assigned a tank destroyer company with M10 American tank destroyers. Combat power included mechanized cavalry troops assigned jeeps with mounting .50 caliber machine guns and 60mm mortars and the M8 greyhound, a light armored car produced by the Ford Motor Company.

Day 1 – August 16

On August 16th, after snipers and fire fight met Granddaddy again on the road back to their command post (CP), he was then off to the town of Le Muy to do some reconnaissance. Then late in the afternoon of August 16th, Truscott ordered his Task Force to begin to assemble to begin executing the prepared plan on the following day.

On August 16th and 17th, there were air drops all around German headquarters LXII Reserve Corps at Draguignan, dispersing it and several hundred German prisoners were captured, including the Corps commanding General of the German LXII Corp (German army General Ferdinand Neuling) and several of his staff. But they managed to escape that day but were taken again two days later along with his entire staff, by Task Force Butler on their first day of operation, seizing another German General officer the next day.

Day 2 - August 17

On August 17th, Truscott received an intercepted message confirming the Germans had received orders to retreat and establish a defensive line in a more favorable terrain away from the beach. The situation was changing quickly.

That same day, Granddaddy was in for instructions. Top secret intelligence discovered 11 Panzer divisions moving to block their advance but not alarmed for even if true, their Corps dispositions can deal with it. An attack was coordinated for 5 am; General Truscott summoned Granddaddy at mid-afternoon to his command post and directed him to march at 6 am the following morning to see how far northward they could get before encountering resistance. Sisterone remained the objective. Granddaddy could choose the route.

Back in Naples, he had tentatively selected the Route Napoleon; It appeared to more direct. But even prior to leaving Naples, He changed the route because he decided that the Route Napoleon was too dangerous. He said 'the terrain was so mountainous that a small enemy force with a single-propelled gun could have made this 'cavalry sweep' just another slow, crawling Italian campaign." Based on the developments, his choice was a sound one.

Truscott said *"You will proceed to Sisteron (a town on the Durance River 90 miles inland) and from there, be prepared to continue north to seize Grenoble or to turn west and seize the high ground north of Montelimar."*

Assembling the Force on the night of August 17-18th, The Task Force Butler briefing took place later that evening at a meeting area near Le Muy.

Day 3- August 18

At dawn on August 18th, Granddaddy started the offensive operations in command of a task force that they had only formed the previous afternoon. They first struck out west in the wake of the 45th Division and then north unopposed into the mountains heading in the general direction of Grenoble.

As they moved out, Granddaddy began to run into stalled columns of soldiers. The problem was at the first bridge out of town. A road block obstruction had been set up by the outposting troops and had to be removed before they could advance. Granddaddy was fuming, He went to the bridge himself and saw that there must have been 200 pounds of TNT in that little bridge-not to mention antitank mines, posts, rails, boulders and cable! It took half the day of feverish work to safely clear the *friendly* obstruction.

84

Then meanwhile on the same day, there was difficulty massing the command from the Argens valley for employment to the northwest or north as planned so Granddaddy decided to assemble his Force at Le Muy in the gap between the 3rd and 45th infantry to drive clear the area between the Durance River and the seacoast. Truscott warned him to prepare the Task Force Butler for another assembly the following day. Granddaddy was on route to Le Muy to survey the location when Truscott encountered him on the road.

In General Truscotts Own Words

*"Had we not planned the organization, assembly, and employment of **Butler Task Force** before we sailed from Naples, we would not have been able to gain the rear of the German XIX Army at Montelimar. That Army then have been able to develop an effective withdrawal and our exploitation would have been far less rapid and extensive. Our assault divisions had been thoroughly trained in rapid movement, and their close pursuit prevented the enemy's withdrawal to even a new defense line. There have been few operations in which the speed of execution has paid greater dividends than in the invasion of southern France".*
– Gen. Lucian K. Truscott Command Mission, 1954

He joined Truscott later that afternoon to report his Force was now gathered at Le Muy except for two units which were expected during the night. They adopted the plan which his staff and he prepared back in Naples for an advance northwest to the Durance

River and then north toward Grenoble or west to seize high ground north of Montelimar to block a German withdrawal through the Montelimar Gap east of the Rhone.

The French Forces of the Interior (the Maquis) in eastern France were especially active in the mountainous areas of the border regions. One German division had been fighting them around Grenoble for weeks. They were so effective that Germans moved only in large groups. The Maquis were provided arms and ammunitions from the United States and England by means of personnel and material parachuted in and officers assisted them in coordinating activities. The Allied forces expected a good deal of help from them and were not disappointed. Their fighting ability was extraordinary, and their knowledge of the country was invaluable.

"Without the Maquis, our mission would have been far more difficult, if indeed impossible", Granddaddy said.

Pilots "would buzz a road' and give his report to the advance echelon commander who then could sweep on if an 'all clear' was the report or act with swiftness where trouble existed'. An observation aircraft did discover a trouble spot south of Quincon where a bridge over a river had been blown up. Granddaddy and his men watched in amazement as hundreds of Maquisards and local townspeople quickly showed up and constructed a ford by placing flagstones flat across the riverbed so that they could continue on and reach Riez at 1800 hours.

So on August 18th, the 4th day after landing, (or D plus 3) at 4 hours before dusk, the operation begins. Task Force Butler secured the town of Reiz with a reconnaissance north of Digne, after advancing 50 miles from their start line, subsequently securing the towns of Sisteron and Apres-Sur Beuch.

At nightfall, things looked very good; they were at Riez with reconnaissance north of Digne.

They had dispersed several enemy detachments and captured more than a thousand prisoners, including the German General (again). Granddaddy would find German General Neuling with his orderly carrying the Generals suitcase, sitting on a park bench, crying, surrounded by tankers holding back the excited mob of French villagers calling for his blood. After receiving the surrender and making a statement, Granddaddy informed the prisoner that he was sending him under officer escort to his corps commander.

The German retreat had split the Americans into 3 different directions. One was the conquest of Toulon and Marseille. Second was Truscott's drive west to push its way towards enemy headquarters.

Then there was Granddaddy and his unopposed march north as he sped northwest, preparing to swing around in front of the Germans. Truscott saw this as an opportunity to direct them behind the German line of withdrawal, the Germans 19th Army could be destroyed and thus avoiding all the tedious fighting that the Italian campaign had fought in so far.

Truscott ordered them to move ahead northward and further clear the way for later assaults.

Day 4 – August 19

By August 19th, Granddaddy's Task Force (to which had been added another battalion) prepared to swing around in front of the Germans.

The men made swift progress. The Task Forces Butlers' motorized units moved up secondary roads in the hills east of the Rhone Valley, quickly reaching Grenoble on the 19th. They were 150 miles from the coast. 230 miles from Lt General Omar Bradley's forces in the North. 200 miles from the German frontier.

By late on the 19th, they were a third of the way there. – Granddaddy and his men reached the Digne-Sisteron region about 50 miles north of the 45th Division and a third of the way to Grenoble. They didn't meet any Germans and were still without a specific mission other than carrying out general reconnaissance.

Still just reconnaissance – no German resistance. If they could get behind German lines, they could destroy German's 19th Army and avoid all the tedious fighting they had encountered in the Italian campaign.

While Headquarters went about the details of outposts, patrols, refilling supplies, prisoner evacuation, checking the town and communications, and coordinating with the Maquis, the

Headquarters cooks got to work making them dinner. It was late before they could eat but what a meal! Granddaddy remembered starting off with a fine French soup, given them by the family whose estate they set up. Then came fried chicken, grand fired potatoes, hot biscuits, a gorgeous salad, crepe suzette, coffee and brandy[27]. The wife and daughter of the estate joined them. These brave ladies were running the farm as the husband-father was absent in Germany. They encountered similar situations a lot. Sometimes the absent one had become a prisoner of war in 1940; sometimes it had been a mere case of kidnapping or forcing the men into military service. Granddaddy said he would like to *'someday to tour that beautiful country and revisit the, I hope, reunited families who befriended us and so many of our aviators who had been forced to land here before liberation.'*

Granddaddy had all his units within his communication but radio contact with the Corps was now out and they were unable to pick up any German traffic. And worse, was that they had run off their maps!

Granddaddy sent Lieutenant Preebles from his staff to Truscott on the 19th to tell him that Saturday they were at Sisteron! Truscott couldn't believe he had made it successfully in such a

---

27 The brandy may have been confiscated from the surrendering German Army – his notes were blurry here.

short amount of time. He seemed genuinely surprised at their rapid success. As if he didn't really have high expectations for them to make it. Or, at least not this quickly.

The Maquis reported German detachments scattered over a wide area from Briancon to Grenoble and were eager to have his support.

General Truscott – In his own words

When I returned to my Command Post (CP) near Vidauban after my conference with General Patch, all but the rear echelon of the command group was in movement to Le Val. Lieutenant Preeble from Butler's staff was waiting for me. Butler was in Sisteron! He had dispersed several enemy detachments and had captured more than a thousand prisoners."

-Truscott

Truscott decided that the time had come to start the 36th Infantry Division north behind him. So he sent Dahlquist to join the Butler Task Force the following day at Sisteron and sent Preebles back to Granddaddy to tell him to remain and wait for him at Sisteron for the elements of the 36th Division to join him and then push reconnaissance to determine the practicability of seizing the Montelimar high north.

But Granddaddy never got the message. The mountains interfered with radio transmissions and Preebles must have been delayed. He was desperate for instructions. The only instructions he received on the night of the 19th restated that the mission of the task force remained unchanged – to continue reconnaissance northward. Shortly before midnight, Granddaddy reported that he intended to continue in the morning. He also reported a shortage of fuel and asked for further instructions, specifically should he head north to Grenoble? or west to Montelimar? Granddaddy was uneasy staying at Sisteron, within enemy territory. There had been reports of a strong German force at Grenoble and one within 30 miles of the Butler Task Force. He was already oriented towards a northward advance but sent his operations officer by liaison plane to Corps headquarters to again request more specific orders.

"In the meantime, orders or no orders, there was work to be done", said Granddaddy later. The artillery cub, used to spot hidden German tanks in the hedgerows, spotted some Germans nearby. He sent a patrol and moving quickly, they gained the pass long in the early afternoon before the Germans approached it.

Day 5 - August 20

Truscott had information that some of the German 11th Panzer Division had crossed the Rhone River and were headed directly for Butlers Task Force but was hesitant to pass along any specific instructions to General Dahlquist, the 36th Division commander while temporarily canceling the northward movement of one 45th regiment complicated matters, leaving the Butler Task Force still without any clear idea of the Germans whereabouts.

In General Truscotts Own Words

"You will move at first light 21 August with all possible speed to Montelimar. Block enemy routes of withdrawal up the Rhone valley in the vicinity. 36th Division follows you".

Gen. Truscott
to Brig. Gen. Federic Butler
At 2045, August 20, 1944

Meanwhile, Granddaddy was increasingly desperate for instructions. As 10 am passed, there were still no orders. Noon and still nothing from either Corps radio or the liaison plane. 2 pm and still no orders.

In the evening of the 20th, Brig. General Robert L. Stack, arrived with some reinforcements. The operations officer returned with the news that further orders would be coming that night. He thought the most logical move was for Butler to head to Grenoble. Then radioing Dahlquist that evening, Stack relayed instructions for Butler to stay around Sisteron until the 36th Division showed up. Dahlquist was concerned with the problems of movement and supply, which were enormous because all units were still at assault scale of transport.

Several hours later, after speaking with Truscott, Dahlquist canceled the move to Grenoble and finally 8:45 pm, Truscott ordered Granddaddy to move as rapidly as possible to Montelimar at dawn the next morning, seize the town, and block the German route of withdrawal. The 36th Division would follow them as soon as possible; Granddaddy would then be attached to the 36th Infantry Division as soon as Dahlquist arrived in the area and could assume control.

Blocking the Montelimar Gap was to be the most important mission. And Granddaddy and his Task Force were being ordered to move directly on the German evacuation route.

Meanwhile, Dahlquist, in his first division command in battle, chose to stay put and not join Granddaddy at Montelimar alarmed after hearing early reports that the enemy was advancing in strength and had so delayed the movement until he could determine the risk. When General Truscott learned of this, he was angry and immediately ordered another command on the way to join Task Force Butler. When they arrived at Montelimar little by little there were many angry communications between Truscott and Dahlquist.

As soon as Truscott returned to his command post, Truscott messaged Dahlquist, reminding him of the orders given him and included:

Dear John:

Grandaddy would say later he and his men could have overtaken and pushed out the Germans sooner had Dahlquists' troops arrived as scheduled, but that 'their resources were extremely limited and everyone was just trying to do their best'.

Soon a call came in that the 11th Panzer Division was south of Durance River. Truscott, Dahlquist and Granddaddy had gone over this problem before and had specific missions to execute but the actual method was left to Granddaddy's own discretion.

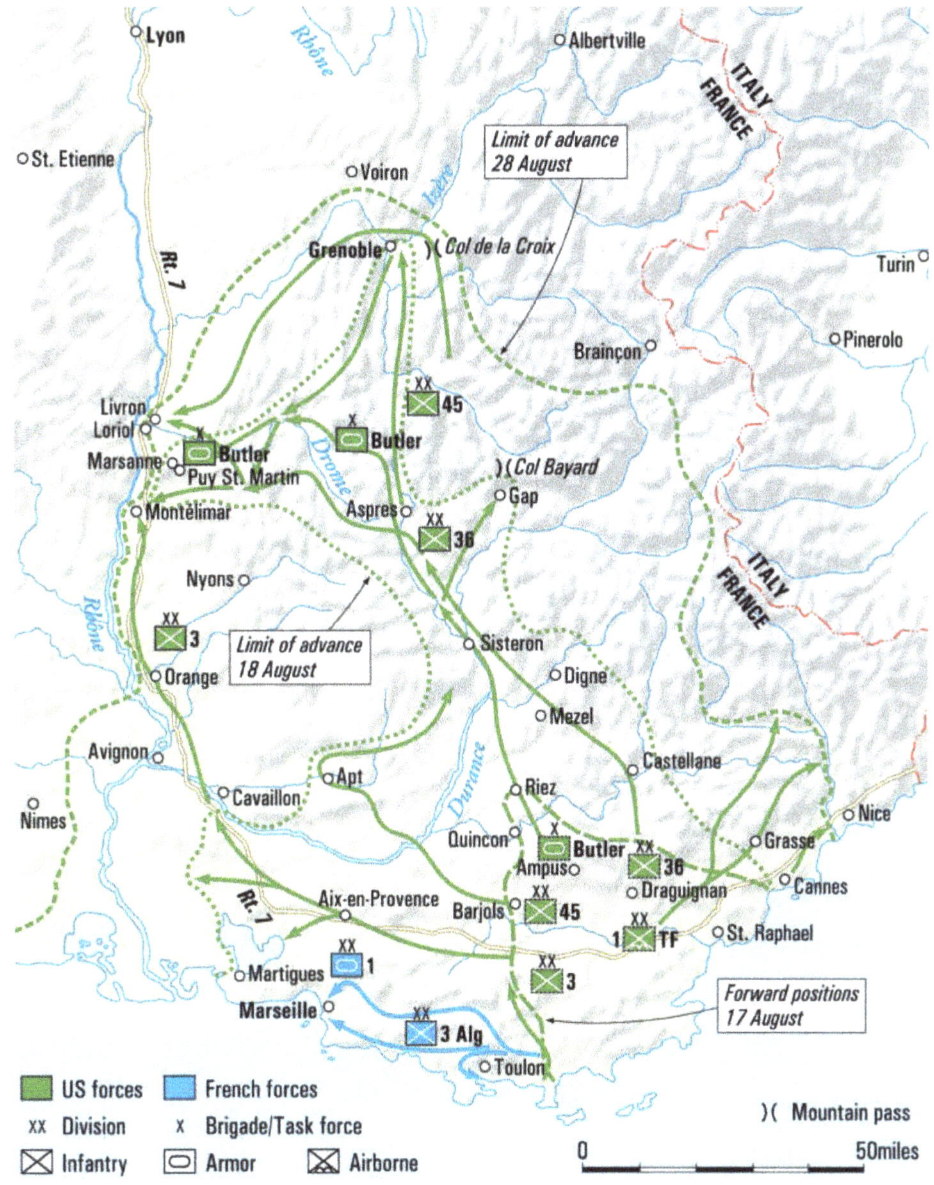

Figure 11 *Task Force Butler was ordered rapidly advance to cut off German retreat from French coast while 36th Division was expected to link up with them ASAP*

Originated as an idea only eighteen days earlier and assembled the afternoon before the attack began, Task Force Butler lacked infantry and ammunitions to physically occupy the road, especially at night.

95

Granddaddy focused their efforts on Hill 300, a sharp north/south ridgeline about four miles north of Montelimar, overlooking the River village of La Concourde's Main road. He established a common post by night into the Condillac Pass area.

Granddaddy's actions on this first day typified the American dilemma. Shooting up whatever attempted to move north of Montelimar during the afternoon of the 20th, they lacked the infantry to physically occupy the road, especially at night, or the munitions to cutting off the highway by fire alone, despite the arrival of two corps artillery battalions sent by Truscott. He had to focus his strength on Hill 300, a sharp north-south ridgeline about 4 miles north of Montelimar, overlooking the main road near the village of La CouCourde. At night, they generally pulled back into the Condillac Pass area, immediately north of Hill 300 where Granddaddy established his command post.

Day 6 – August 21 (Montelimar)

Early on the 21st, Granddaddy received written instructions to attack 90 miles west to seize high ground above the City of Montelimar but not the City itself. And to do it before darkness. Truscott was also sending two artillery battalions and the remainder of the 143rd regiment for battle support.

These instructions required American tanks, trucks and howitzers to rapidly conduct a long-distance road march through hostile territory. The route lay over a formidable mountain range with a twisty road cut into the side of the cliffs; Movement off the road would have been impossible. Granddaddys Task Forces'

96

path could have been blocked in any one of scores of places..., but thankfully no enemy action had yet developed, nor had demolitions been emplaced.

The Task Force had been oriented towards Grenoble (north) but now had to regroup. Some had to stay behind to secure the rear but by the end of the day, the bulk of the task force team was within 13 miles of the Rhone River at the town of Crest.

Overcoming enormous challenges, they prepared themselves to meet the dreaded German Mark V Panther tanks that awaited them at the crossroads town named Montelimar. Unknown to the German commanders but ultimately a very big deal were the actions of Granddaddy's quickly assembled task force.

Granddaddys' ad hoc group of men and officers quickly forced their way through the rugged hills of Provence and unblocked into the Rhone Valley on August 21, just barely ahead of the retreating Germans.

The Montelimar attack began on the morning of the 21st and immediately received reports of an enemy nearby. Granddaddy responded with strength to discourage the enemy by securing the passes and lines of communication, leaving behind most of their armor.

'Later when skirmishes and rapid advances piled the two armies together in the Battle of Montelimar, this sensibly pleasant

process of war naturally gave way to killing and torture", Granddaddy wrote later.

On the afternoon of August 21st, Granddaddy – deep behind enemy lines, following a 90-mile road march over heavily forested, narrow mountainous terrain - reached the vicinity of Marsanne and placed artillery in position to fire on Highway 7. He tried to capture Montelimar but was repulsed. The Germans had seized the vital terrain north of Montelimar, including the long ridge on the high ground.

On the same day, Task Force Butler reached high ground of Montelimar, surprising Germans retreating north along the highway, resulting in heavy enemy casualties. The next two days would be spent trying desperately to hold onto the high ground, waiting for the reinforcements and supplies promised to arrive to continue offensive operations.

Just before midnight on the 21st, Granddaddy radioed Truscott to report the Task force's completion of its assignment. Granddaddy said his forces were thinly spread out, but with some help, he could not only hold on but could successfully attack Montelimar the next afternoon.

Suffering from fatigue from third day and night of continuous attacks repeatedly against the larger enemy forces and superior tanks, withstanding the ferocious attacks of a large force of a German Panzer division and with a shortage of trucks and fuel, no ammunition, food, or water and many wounded in need of medical attention, while completely surrounded by an overwhelming German force – with no knowledge of when anything or anybody would arrive - Granddaddy maintained that they could hold out if reinforcements would arrive.

 But could his small, thinly-spread command hold on until help arrived?

By the next morning, neither reinforcements nor supplies had arrived.

Day 7 – August 22

Then Germans struck.

On the 22nd, some of the Task Force Butler were already scattered between Aspres and the Town of Gap, a sizeable town surrounded by hills, and 20-30 miles above Sisteron and better oriented for an advance north to Grenoble than for a dash west to the Rhone. They were further delayed by incessant communications problems in the rough Maritime Alps, where towns and roads were generally located in the deep valleys. There were ongoing fuel and vehicle shortages. Capturing German fuel helped them put their force and one other 36th Division battalion in the Montelimar region by the evening of the 22nd but most of the American infantry had to move north in a complex and time-consuming series of foot marches and truck shuttles.

These two critical days, as reinforcements arrived, became known as the "Battle at the Square" or "Montelimar Battle Square" in the Town of Crest.

They could not hold the main east bank highway along the Rhone during the day on the 22nd, but little lived to escape on that road either. Artillery covered the road, tanks, tank destroyers, armored cars, even ground mounted 57mm infantry guns were pouring aimed fire at the dense traffic. And by excellent shooting and good luck, they bagged several trains and railway on the east bank was blocked.

German Tanks had begun arriving at Montelimar on August 22nd, attacking from two directions, launching an immediate attack, moving east along the southern bank of the Roubion and then striking north behind the Task Force.

The Germans were probing everywhere. Early in the afternoon the Task Force got a real scare. Five Mark tanks, supported by panzer grenadiers succeeded in crossing the Roubion near Cleon. Troop A fought skillfully, knocking out several of the supporting vehicles, but became cut off and surrounded. This was the time and place to use Granddaddy's reserves and, anticipating enemy power in the area, this was the location. He had picked out the site from which the reserve was to operate. But the slowness of the relief at the Gap had delayed this vital element of the command. It was still on the road. Fortunately, the tank destroyers that Felber had did excellent work and stemmed the advance. More power was needed. One platoon of Troop A still was cut off and had lost two armored cars and three jeeps. Due to the hilly nature of southern France, they could not raise their advancing column by radio. Its commanding officer had driven ahead and was at the Command Post. Now the Germans were between them and his troops. He estimated the column of marching soldiers could not be more than thirty minutes from the point where they would contact the enemy. 'Forewarned would be forearmed', Granddaddy said. Their only chance of communication was a dropped message from a cub plane. An artillery plane was called in, given the message, dropped it, and rescue columns arrived for what would be called a 'movie finish'.

In the words of Brig. General Frederic Butler
"It is was a movie finish" with destroyed German tanks and trucks burning and their infantry driven back."

-       Brig. Gen. Frederic Butler (about the German retreat from Montelimar on August 22, 1944)

The German tanks which had crossed the Roubion were destroyed, the infantry were driven back and on the south bank, several fires burned merrily where the task force guns had found trucks and light vehicles. It was a good honest fight. The reserve had arrived in the nick of time." [28]

Some of Task Force late armored units left to guard the rear at the town of Gap, had been relieved by

---

28 Task Force Butler, by FBB

the anticipated 36th Division arrivals from Sisteron and helped to throw back this dangerous thrust, arriving in time to successfully counterattack.

As it turned out, the small armored German team that was reported to Truscott earlier had been merely a ruse, something to keep the Americans guessing so now the Germans would have a difficult time moving their armor north to fight around Montelimar.

Occupying a defensive position, Dalquist finally arrived on the morning of August 23rd, intermingling with them over a wide area. Then he disbanded Task Force Butler, returning elements to their parent units.

Day 8 – August 23

Dahlquist assumed Granddaddy's command on the 23rd and was repeatedly attacked and counterattacked with greater strength. Task Force Butler kept fighting until under control later that day. The deactivation was temporary; Task Force Butler was soon reconstituted with a new mission.

The Germans were finally able to clear the western slopes of Hill 300 of Americans to the north, opening the roads, allowing the German to leave again. They had been driven back and were retreating.

As Granddaddy said later that **"it is was a movie finish"** with destroyed German tanks, burning trucks, and their infantry driven back.

On August 23rd, Granddaddy handwrote a message to Truscott that he received in the late afternoon reporting his situation north of Montelimar:

"Gen. Truscott –

"We have a much-improved position today. Have gained more high ground north of Montelimar and are getting into position to clean up the latter place this afternoon.

"Column of about 50-60 vehicles, including a few tanks hit us at 0600 this morning. Road block and reconnaissance held, artillery did its stuff, and now the reserve (1 tank company and 1 infantry company) are pursuing. Apparently Jerry is hurt plenty. Yesterday over 100 vehicles destroyed and two trains were hit and badly messed up. TD's and tanks have direct fire positions on roads north of Montelimar.

"About 30 missing in yesterday's mix up at Puy St. Martin, lost one tank, one light tank, and two armored vehicles. K and W about 10. Jerry took a polishing.

"A Panzer officer captured today has a fund of information, summary of which is going back by plane herewith.

FBB"

Ultimately the ensuing struggle around Montelimar pitted them against von Wietersheims panzers and surviving infantry divisions of the Germans' 19th Army as they arrived northward. The battle lasted nine days – with Task Force Buter in constant combat from the 25th -29th. and both sides are committing increasingly larger forces against the other with indecisive results. The retreating German units ultimately forced their way to Lyon but suffered horrendous casualties in the process.

Day 9 - August 24

On August 24th, and to Truscott's dismay, Dahlquist is absent from the Gap. Apparently, he had delayed movement until he could determine extent of reports of heavy enemy advance and strength. So an angry Truscott sent other troops to join them.

"2 Battalions of 141 now in. Third reported in route. 142 is headed for Lyons and I have a plane out hunting for them. 131 artillery is here."

And German columns are still moving north on both sides of the Rhone, despite their blockade North of Montelimar. Truscott met with Dahlquist, Stack and Granddaddy.

Day 10 August 25

On August 25th, General Patch issued orders to continue to advance north to join up with General Patton's 3rd Army.

After Truscott directed Dahlquist on August 25th to reassemble Task Force Butler by dark that day so to have strong striking force in Division reserve, Granddaddy was sent through to Grane to clear the Loriol situation. News of enemy advance E to Grane from Loriol. Germans continuing to withdraw to the north in spite of Dahlquists assurances their block on Highway 7 was effective. During the afternoon, they stopped the Germans from attacking eastward from Loriol toward Crest.

Truscott visited Granddaddy and some of the Task Force (a battalion of the 143rd Infantry and elements of the 141st Infantry) in a jeep at Condillac to survey damages. Heavy fighting was in progress on the ridges. The heaviest fighting in the CouCourde is where Granddaddy was trying to reestablish the block on Highway 7. Truscott left late afternoon by jeep in a driving mountain storm.

So the Butler Task Force had existed for 14 days, advanced over 235 miles, liberated approximately 6,645 square miles of southern France, **captured more than 3500 German prisoners** (including 3 generals) and destroyed hundreds of German vehicles. Even more amazing, the Task Force seized a key piece of terrain along the enemies withdrawal line and held it until reinforcements arrived two days later, marking the beginning of the 8-day battle of Montelimar in France.

It's amazing what they accomplished. On August 18th, the attack commenced in the early morning. On August 20th, their unit marched 90 miles over mountainous terrain and heavily forested roads, pursuing retreating Germans. Granddaddys skillful offensive use of cavalry was matched by the defensive employment of his command the following day at Montelimar. The Task Force attacked over 200 miles into the enemy rear to seize high ground, overlooking highway N-7, north of Montelimar, assisting US VI Corps to maneuver the German 19th Army into a narrow escape corridor.

Day 11 August 26

By early on the 26th, not much had been accomplished by either side. The Germans had opened the road but that was all they had accomplished. They were spread out, vulnerable to attack at weak points.

On August 26th, Truscott ordered more troops to the "battle square area". The only attack Dahlquist had planned for the day was to send Task Force Butler to attack the Condilac Pass to restore the roadblock with rifle companies and some tanks. They ran into Germans both moving up from the south and attacking down from the north, thwarting the attacks, barely hanging onto the Hill 300 after being pushed off the road.

Days 12-13 August 27-28

August 27th and 28th, the heavy fighting continued near Montelimar. "Carnage Compounded". Direct and tank steady stream of fire. Motionless enemy vehicles, jamming up bumper to bumper along Highway 7 between Montelimar and Loriol fighter bombers pounded German escape routes. South of Montelimar, two Battalion Infantry surrounded and captured a
106

double banked column of appx. 350 German guns and vehicles which were stretched along the highway over 2 kilometers. Most of the German tanks had broken through the Task Forces' block, escaping their trap but not as bad as it first seemed. Yet there were hundreds of dead horses and dead bodies. Engineers with bulldozers had to clear the road before they could use them. It was an awful sight. And terrible stench.

Truscott said *"I know of no place where more damage was inflicted upon our troops in the field[29]"* and almost entirely by ground weapons, artillery, tanks, tank destroyers and demolitions. There was not a lot of air support because of the lack of forward ground control (i.e. no briefed missions or armed reconnaissance).

On the 28th, Germans doubled down to clear Americans from the area and surrounded Americans. However, somehow Dalquist avoided encirclement.

Day 14: August 29

On August 29th, the final attack succeeded in liberating the City of Montelimar and the Town of Loriol and capturing 55 German soldiers.

---

[29] Truscott, Command Missions, Page 275

On August 30th, as the 3rd and 35th Infantry Divisions were mopping up German remnants in the Montelimar battle square and 14 days after it was first assembled, the Task Force Butler was dissolved for the last time.

The success of Task Force Butlers' victory was made doubly sweet by contrast to the protracted agony and frustrations of Cassino and the Anzio beachhead. Sweet victory as it should be. Swift and complete.

Montelimar netted 5000 prisoners, destroyed more than 4000 vehicles and eliminated the 3 38th and 189th German Divisions.

In 14 days, at a cost of 1331 killed and wounded, 23,000 prisoners They had liberated Montelimar and so many other towns and villages along the way.

As Granddaddys command car entered the French village of Quincon in August 1944, he said **_This was war deluxe._** Jubilant civilians filled the streets, tossing flowers, fruit and bottles of wine to the passing American G.I.'s who had just liberated them from two years of brutal German occupation.

He appreciated their emulations, wishing these celebrating villagers to move to clear a path so his tanks and trucks could keep moving forward. The warm August sun was growing low in the sky, and he still had many miles to go that night.

Things had gone well for them the first day of their mission. The enemy had been bowled over by surprise and was proving not too tough. The weather was excellent, roads ok, and minimal resistance. By dusk, Granddaddys' 3,000 men and 1,000 vehicles would dash 45 miles behind enemy lines without suffering a single casualty.

In the Words of the U.S. Army

"The Task Force Butler operation certainly one of the most colorful and dashing ventures of the entire war, went almost unnoticed"

"The [second] beach invasion in Southern France and Task Force Butler did not receive the attention in the pressor from historians as the Normandy invasion or even the Italian Campaign."

So in just 14 days TFB attack advanced 235 miles from Allied front lines to seize terrain that dominated the German 19th Army's withdrawal routes. During its advance it liberated nearly 6,645 square miles of southern France, including 7 towns and small cities, small towns and villages. It was directly responsible of the capture of 3500 men.

Summary of Accomplishments:

- ➢ Under 14 days without ever training together, advanced 235 miles from allied front lines to seize ground that dominated the German 19th Army's' withdrawal routes.
- ➢ Liberated an estimated 6,645 square miles of southern France including 7 large towns and many small cities, towns and villages.
- ➢ Captured over 3500 Germans alive (including 3 Generals) while suffering only 15 casualties
- ➢ Destroyed or captured thousands of combat vehicles
- ➢ Had a positive dramatic strategic effect on the course of the campaign
- ➢ Increased momentum and speed of the Germans' withdrawal from southern France

Granddaddys' task force carried out a German 19th Army ambush in what would be called *'one of the most successful operational pursuits of World War II'.[30]*

In the 34th Infantry Division, Granddaddy would be awarded both the Distinguished Service Cross for Army service for actions during World War II in October 1943 and the Legion of Merit for service from 1944-1945.

---

30 Task Force Butler, Michael J. Volpe (2)

Chapter 5:
Awards and medals
WWII efforts

AWARDS & MEDALS

- Distinguished Service Cross

- Legion of Merit, the Oak Leaf Cluster

- Bronze Star

- Purple Heart

- Combat Infantry Badge

- Croix de Guerre with Pal (France)

- Legion of Honor (France)

- Cross of Valor (Italy)

- Knights of the Sovereign Military Order of Malta by Pope John XXIII, 1962
- His Alma Mater, St. Ignatius High School Alumni Association gave him the Christ the King award in 1965.
- USF Honorary Degree of Doctorate at Law 1948

January 20, 1944

FREDERICK B. BUTLER, (012047), Colonel, Infantry, Commanding Officer ***Infantry Regiment, for extraordinary heroism in action. From *** to ***October 1943, Colonel BUTLER led his command to each succeeding objective, in its advance from *** to ***, Italy, displaying aggressive and inspirational leadership of the highest order. On *** October, when the *** Battalion of his Regiment was ordered to make a crucial attack near ***, he came forward and accompanied these troops on their mission, encouraging them to greater efforts. Again on ***October, when one of his battalions was halted by enemy fire near ***, he personally rallied the officers and men, within full view of the enemy and under continuous small arms fire and organized a successful resumption of the attack. Colonel Butler has continually exposed himself to enemy fire, without regard to his personal welfare, in order to inspire the members of his command. His presence in the front lines and his close contact with the advance elements of his command exemplify his fearlessness, aggressiveness and complete devotion to duty.

Distinguished Service Cross

AWARDED FOR ACTIONS
DURING World War II

Service: Army

Division: 34th Infantry Division

GENERAL ORDERS:

Headquarters, Fifth U.S. Army, General Orders No. 9 (1944)

CITATION:

(Citation Needed) - SYNOPSIS: The President of the United States of America, authorized by Act of Congress July 9, 1918, takes pleasure in presenting the Distinguished Service Cross to Colonel (Infantry) Frederic Bates Butler, United States Army, for extraordinary heroism in connection with military operations against an armed enemy while serving with the 168th Infantry Regiment, 34th Infantry Division, in action against enemy forces in October 1943. Colonel Butler's outstanding leadership, personal bravery and zealous devotion to duty exemplify the highest traditions of the military forces of the United States and reflect great credit upon himself, the 34th Infantry Division, and the United States Army.

Legion of Merit

AWARDED FOR ACTIONS
DURING World War II

Service: Army

Rank: Colonel

Division: 34th Infantry Division

GENERAL ORDERS:

Unites States Military Academy Register of Graduates

CITATION:

(Citation Needed) - SYNOPSIS: Colonel (Infantry) Frederic Bates Butler, United States Army, was awarded the Legion of Merit for exceptionally meritorious conduct in the performance of outstanding services to the Government of the United States while serving with the 168th Infantry Regiment, 34th Infantry Division from 1944 to 1945.

Chapter 6:
After the War (1945)

Granddaddy was wounded and returned home before the Battle of the Bulge[31] in 1945.

During the Korean War from 1950-1953, he was chief of staff of Army Forces in the Far East.

From 1945-46, he was commissioner for Australia and South Pacific Foreign Liquidation Commission. 1946-47, he was U.S. Army in Seoul Korea. From 1947-49, he was in the 6th Army Sixth Army Engineer San Francisco Commanding General. He wrote a two-part account of his Task Force Butler experience from memory while crossing the Pacific in 1946 and lent it to the Army Historical Division for research with permission to edit and publish. In 1949-50, he oversaw the construction of the military garrison at Entwetok, following a battle of the Pacific campaign of the War, fought in February 1944. The Entewok is a large coral atoll of 40 islands in the Pacific Ocean where on November 1st, 1952, the U.S. detonated the world's first hydrogen bomb.

He took charge as commanding General from 1950-52 of an infantry training camp in East Texas at Camp Fannin and Camp Howze. From May

---

31 Also known as the Ardennes Offensive, the Battle of the Bulge was the last major German offensive campaign on the Western Front during the World War II, taking place from 16 December 1944 to 25 January 1945. It was launched through the densely forested Ardennes region between Belgium and Luxemburg.

24, 1951 through February 6, 1952, at Camp Fort McCoy and Fort Leonard Wood in Texas, he was Commander of the training center during the Korean War.

History Center Photo

New commander ...

Brig. Gen. Frederic B. Butler (second from left) takes command at Camp McCoy May 24, 1951. Butler served as Camp McCoy commander through Feb. 6, 1952. Fort McCoy is celebrating "A Century of Service" throughout 2009.

His nephew Lewis visited him at the training camp in Texas. The Battle of the Bulge was going on about this time, and it was over by then. January and February 1945. And he had been wounded,

116

and his division kept on fighting. Not sure if they got involved in the Battle of the Bulge or not. But anyway, he was home. And of course, Lewis hadn't seen him; he'd left home in 1942, for the invasion of North Africa, and gone through Italy and the South of France.

 So Lewis came to visit him in an infantry training camp in East Texas, that he was then the general in charge of. And Lewis was just delighted to see him. And he thinks he spent two nights there. But that's when it only finally occurred to Lewis that this war was really tough.

Lewis would say later about his impressions from the visit that *'You read about it, but— they were training, doing night training with live fire. About every fifth bullet in the machine gun would be fired about three feet off the ground, and they were training guys to crawl under that fire. And if they made a mistake, they were going to get killed in the training. And so they learned to crawl pretty well, especially since there were tracers going over their head. I'd go out with my uncle Fred, and I remember we stopped in the dead of night by a foxhole, and my uncle said to a man in the foxhole, "How you doing, soldier?" And I guess the soldier couldn't see his stars as a general, but he knew that this was an older guy that was an officer, and he says, "I'm fine, sir. Fine, sir." And so I was watching my uncle be an army officer, which I'd never really seen before. '*

'And all I remember is him saying something to me sort of offhand about it after that, like, if they don't get trained well here, they'll be dead in two weeks. Because the casualty rates in the infantry are enormous in the first couple weeks, with new— **And he'd gone through three years of seeing people killed.** *So that was that. '*

-Lewis Butler, 2009

The next day, Lewis joined him to observe some soldier training exercises —when infantry advances, there is supporting fire that's sort of rolling fire that goes over their heads, so it's hitting the enemy fifty or a hundred yards in front of them. And they had a place where they were training the troops to advance, with artillery shells coming over their head, and a little grandstand. And Granddaddy is the commanding general and can tell Lewis is trying hard to keep his mouth shut. He is just a spectator. And somebody made a mistake, and in this 75mm howitzer or 44 whatever it was, put in one bag of powder too little. And so the shell went out and landed right in the middle of the troops that were being trained. These were live shells. Fortunately, the shell went into a previous shell hole, because the whole place was nothing but shell holes; they'd been doing this exercise for

118

months, if not years. And it went into the shell hole, and the shell hole was full of water. So this giant geyser of water went up in the air. And when it all cleared, and the smoke and everything else, nobody was injured. And Granddaddy was so angry! He was just livid! But he didn't start yelling. He just started talking in his steeliest voice. And Lewis is there as a spectator. Granddaddy went around to the captain that oversaw the artillery and spoke very clearly to him about what just happened and he looked understandably terrified. And then Granddaddy said, *"I will see you at five o'clock tomorrow morning."* He was furious. Well, Lewis remained with him without words. They didn't speak of it again. There was no discussion that either remembers. And so the next morning, Granddaddy gets up and goes alone for this meeting at 5:00 a.m., and Lewis meets him for breakfast at 6:00 a.m. And he gets there and he doesn't say much about it, but there are a bunch of officers standing around. And they all look like they'd expected to go before a firing squad at 5:00 a.m.; Granddaddy had chewed them up one side and down another. He hoped Lewis understood his anger.

There can be no joking; No softness in training or on the battlefield. He really just wants them all to come home in one piece. He said to Lewis that *"Ineptitude can not tolerated—it will get them -and their brothers - killed.'*

Then a heavy guy that was a lieutenant or a captain passes by and he looked at him and said *"You better get about twenty pounds off your butt if you want to fight in Europe"*.

Then Granddaddy took Lewis to the train and off he went.

In 1953, the Butlers lived in Japan while Granddaddy was chief of staff US Air Force as Japan Logistical Command until his retirement for physical disability in April 1953. Here Mom would collect Japanese treasures, and brought home her Geisha dolls, scrolls, old antique parchment paper umbrellas, and Imari china plates and tableware.

Granddaddy visited Lewis after the war at his prep school to see how he was doing. And they went to a football game. It was in November, and one of his friends had a flask of whiskey at the game. And he's passing it around to everyone but Granddaddy. All are taking nips at the game. So anyway, he didn't get the nip of whiskey
"Listen. This is my uncle." Lewis tells his friend.
That was part of the tradition of prep school. Silver flask, curved silver flask, put it in your back pocket. It was like The Great Gatsby. So as soon thereafter, Granddaddy wrote Lucy telling her. "Well, I had a great time with Lewis at the football game, but I was dying to have a drink and they kept hiding this flask and I never got a nip."
By that time, he was out of the Army and was General Manager of the new airport in San Francisco and S.F. Fire Commissioner even though he never liked politics. And that's a political job. And after he finished building the new airport buildings and the roof was on, he finally just quit. And they had a going-away press

conference when he said absolutely nothing. The Chronicle reporter covering it told Lewis, "Your uncle's wonderful."

They'd ask him questions. "Did you enjoy the job?"

"Yes."

"Are you going to miss it?"

"No."

"What are you going to do?"

"I don't know."

Lewis finally graduated from Princeton, and his mother and brother came back and met him and they drove home. And by that time, he'd taken the law school aptitude test, the first year they gave it, and Lewis signed up to go to Stanford Law School.

Retired (1953)

He retired from the Army in 1953, returning to his home in San Francisco.

Frederic Bates Butler served as a member of the San Francisco Fire Commission briefly upon retiring, resigning after being appointed manager of San Francisco International Airport. He served more than three years, a time when a $25 million bond issue was passed by voters to finance expansion of the airport. He said ' *the 10-year construction program envisaged under the bond issue should be undertaken by a younger man.'*

1954- 1960 General Manager of the San Francisco International Airport (when they moved Mills Field out to what's now SFO.) Commissioner of San Francisco Fire Department

1953-1957 SFO Airport Director

Figure 12 San Francisco Airport flysfo.com 8.24 SFO

SFO Airport Manager

1956

After retirement from San Francisco government in 1956, he served on the board of directors of St. Mary's Hospital and was active in the United Crusade and the Boy Scouts of America. He was also a member of the Bohemian Club and the Knights of Malta.

His daughter Popsy (Mom) married to Robert Joseph Henderson (Dad) from San Jose California on February 11th, 1956.

Figure 13 Grandmommy & Granddaddy at our parents Henderson Wedding 1956

Figure 14 Mom and Dads Wedding 1956

1964

He and Herbert Hoover had stayed in touch and continued to have talks.

Our grandparents would have their last visit with him in New York at the Waldorf in early September 1964. They had just come back from Europe. Granddaddy had been invited by the French Government to participate in an official mission in France. On their return, they enjoyed a brief visit with 90-year-old Mr. Hoover. He remembered it distinctly.

124

'When it was time for us to leave and we started to make our way to the door of the apartment. I turned and said to Mr. Hoover, who was sitting in his wheelchair,

'We missed you at the Grove this summer, Mr. Hoover, and it wasn't only your close friends; it was everybody.'

He said, Well, I was sorry I couldn't go. You know, the Grove is the one thing I'm going to miss very much."

I said, "Oh, Mr. Hoover, that's the way we all feel now and then; that's the everybody feels."

And then I reached out to really take my leave and shake his hand, the way that he held my hand and the feeble pressure that he exerted – I suppose it was all the pressure he could muster – indicated to me very definitely, without a spoken word, that he was saying "goodbye".

He (Mr. Hoover) was not a man to complain about his condition or anything like that, but he was a realist and at 90 years old, I guess these things become inevitable.

As Granddaddy said later when asked about the inevitability of death, **'Well, every day you live it's one day closer.'**

Hoover died about six or seven weeks later.

1974

In 1974, our grandparents celebrated their 50th Golden Wedding anniversary at the Bohemian Club in San Francisco. Black Tie. No gifts or flowers please.

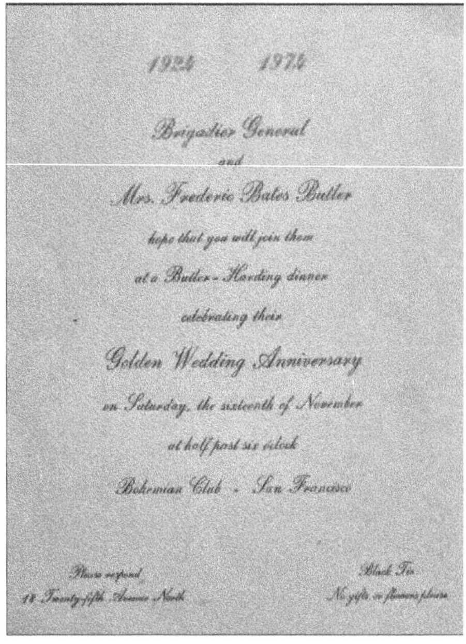

Figure 15 50th Wedding Celebration Invite

1984

Grandmommy died after a long illness. She was 84.

1987

Granddaddy died at home after a long illness. He was 90.

Private services were held for Army Brigadier General Frederick B. Butler, 90, who died at his home on Saturday June 20th 1987 after a long illness.

Authors Note

Nearly a decade after Granddaddy passed away, my company Henderson Capital Partners was selected as a co-managing underwriter on a $106 million SFO Special Facility 1997 Lease Revenue Bond Issue. As the firms lead investment banker, I attended all the finance team meetings held in the administrative offices on the 3rd floor at SFO to work on the deal structure and negotiate the financing terms. Surrounded by all senior male investment bankers from Smith Barney and the Airports finance officers, as well as legal counsels, I was in stunned awe to discover Granddaddy's large, framed portrait on the boardroom wall amongst all the other previous general managers, wondering if he was responsible for Butler Field naming rights too (which he wasn't). I was so proud; I couldn't shake his presence with me the entire afternoon. I mentioned it casually while shaking hands with the General Manager at the end of the meeting and gained a new subtle respect and acceptance from all around the table from thereon.

$105,610,000

AIRPORT COMMISSION OF THE CITY AND COUNTY OF SAN FRANCISCO
SAN FRANCISCO INTERNATIONAL AIRPORT
SPECIAL FACILITIES LEASE REVENUE BONDS
(SFO FUEL COMPANY LLC)

$93,355,000	$12,255,000
SERIES 1997A (AMT)	**SERIES 1997B (TAXABLE)**

Dated: September 1, 1997   **Due: January 1, as shown on the inside front cover**

The Special Facilities Lease Revenue Bonds (SFO FUEL COMPANY LLC) are being issued by the Airport Commission of the City and County of San Francisco in two separate series, consisting of Series A and Series B. The 1997 Bonds will mature in the years and the principal amounts, and shall bear interest at the rates, shown on the inside front cover. Interest on the 1997 Bonds will be payable semiannually on each January 1 and July 1, commencing January 1, 1998. The 1997 Bonds will be delivered in fully registered form only, and, when issued, will be registered in the name of CEDE & Co., as nominee of The Depository Trust Company, New York, New York. DTC will act as securities depository of the 1997 Bonds. Ownership interests in the 1997 Bonds may be purchased in book-entry form only, in the denominations of $5,000 and integral multiples thereof. Purchasers will not receive physical certificates representing their ownership interests in the 1997 Bonds.

The 1997 Bonds are being issued to finance certain additions and improvements to jet fuel and gasoline delivery facilities serving domestic and international air carriers and ground service equipment users operating at San Francisco International Airport. The 1997 Bonds are limited obligations of the Airport Commission and will be payable as to principal thereof, and interest and premium, if any, thereon, solely from certain amounts ("Facilities Rent") payable to the Airport Commission pursuant to a Fuel System Lease, dated as of September 1, 1997 with SFO FUEL COMPANY LLC, which amounts have been assigned to BNY Western Trust Company, as Trustee, and pledged therefor as described herein, and from amounts on deposit in certain funds and accounts created under the Trust Agreement, dated as of May 1, 1997, between the Airport Commission and the Trustee. SFO FUEL COMPANY LLC is a Delaware limited liability company, the members of which are certain air carriers operating at San Francisco International Airport. Payments of principal of, and interest and premium, if any, on the 1997 Bonds will be guaranteed by

SFO FUEL COMPANY LLC

pursuant to a Guaranty Agreement, dated as of September 1, 1997, between the Company and the Trustee. The Company was formed solely for the purpose of leasing, financing, improving, operating and maintaining the fuel delivery system at the Airport. Pursuant to an Amended and Restated Fuel System Interline Agreement, dated as of September 1, 1997, among the Company and certain Contracting Airlines serving the Airport, the Contracting Airlines are obligated to make payments each month to the Company which in the aggregate are sufficient, together with payments received by the Company from other users of the fuel and gasoline delivery system at the Airport, to pay all costs of the Company, including Facilities Rent in an amount equal to principal of, premium, if any, and interest on the 1997 Bonds.

The 1997 Bonds will be subject to optional, mandatory and extraordinary redemption prior to maturity as more fully described herein.

The 1997 Bonds are special limited obligations of the Airport Commission payable as to principal thereof, premium, if any, and interest thereon, solely from the Trust Estate. The 1997 Bonds will not constitute a general obligation of, or be secured by, a pledge of, the faith and credit or the taxing power of the City, the State of California, or any political subdivision of the State. The 1997 Bonds will not constitute an indebtedness of the Airport Commission except to the extent provided in the Trust Agreement. Neither the State of California, any political subdivision of the State of California, nor the City (other than the Airport Commission) will be obligated to pay the principal of, premium, if any, or interest on the 1997 Bonds, or other costs incident thereto. The Airport Commission will be obligated to make such payments only from the Facilities Rent and other amounts pledged therefor pursuant to the Trust Agreement.

Payment of the principal of and interest on the 1997 Bonds when due will be insured by a municipal bond insurance policy to be issued by Ambac Assurance Corporation simultaneously with the delivery of the 1997 Bonds.

Ambac

In the opinion of Orrick, Herrington & Sutcliffe LLP and Pamela S. Jue, Attorney at Law, Co-Bond Counsel, based upon an analysis of existing laws, regulations, rulings and court decisions, and assuming, among other matters, compliance with certain covenants, interest on the Series A Bonds is excluded from gross income for federal income tax purposes under Section 103 of the Internal Revenue Code of 1986 (the "Code"), except that no opinion is expressed as to the status of interest on any Series A Bond during any period such Series A Bond is held by a person who is a "substantial user" of the facilities financed by the 1997 Bonds or is a "related person" within the meaning of Section 147(a) of the Code. Co-Bond Counsel observe, however, that interest on the Series A Bonds is a specific preference item for purposes of the federal individual and corporate alternative minimum taxes. Interest on the Series B Bonds is not excluded from gross income for federal income tax purposes. In the further opinion of Co-Bond Counsel, interest on the 1997 Bonds is exempt from State of California personal income taxes. Co-Bond Counsel express no opinion regarding other tax consequences relating to the ownership or disposition of, or the accrual or receipt of interest on, the 1997 Bonds. See "TAX MATTERS" herein.

THIS COVER PAGE CONTAINS CERTAIN INFORMATION FOR GENERAL REFERENCE ONLY. IT IS NOT INTENDED TO BE A SUMMARY OF THE SECURITY FOR OR TERMS OF THIS ISSUE. INVESTORS ARE ADVISED TO READ THE ENTIRE OFFICIAL STATEMENT TO OBTAIN INFORMATION ESSENTIAL TO THE MAKING OF AN INFORMED INVESTMENT DECISION. CAPITALIZED TERMS USED ON THIS COVER PAGE NOT OTHERWISE DEFINED SHALL HAVE THE MEANINGS SET FORTH HEREIN.

The 1997 Bonds are offered when, as and if issued by the Airport Commission and delivered to the Underwriters, subject to the approval of legality thereof by Orrick, Herrington & Sutcliffe LLP and Pamela S. Jue, Attorney at Law, Co-Bond Counsel, and certain other conditions. Certain legal matters will be passed upon for the Airport Commission by the City Attorney, for SFO FUEL COMPANY LLC by Sherman & Howard LLC, Denver, Colorado and Elliman Burke Hoffman & Johnson, San Francisco, California, for the Underwriters by Stradling, Yocca, Carlson & Rauth, a Professional Corporation, San Francisco, California, and Lofton, De Lancie & Nelson, San Francisco, California, Co-Underwriters' Counsel, for the trustee by Lillick & Charles LLP, San Francisco, California, and for Ambac Assurance Corporation by its counsel. It is expected that delivery of the 1997 Bonds will occur through the DTC book-entry system in New York, New York on or about October 7, 1997.

Smith Barney Inc.   Henderson Capital Partners, Inc.

EPILOGUE

After the War, we now know that he would never talk about it.

However, plenty has been publicly written if you look hard enough.

And although he would never talk about it, he was certainly referenced quite a bit in stories about during those 2 weeks in Southern France during the second World War.

Retired and back at his west coast home, built in 127, in the wealthy enclave of the Seacliff neighborhood of San Francisco, California on the northern tip of the San Francisco Peninsula and less than a mile away from the Presidio (a U.S. Army base), he refused to engage in conversations about the war. He would spend most of his days and evenings in his combination sitting room, and book-lined library at his large mahogany desk in his leather chair of his home, gazing at the awesome Golden Gate Bridge and the lovely Baker Beach, surrounded by magazines, newspapers, books. He kept up with current events. A news junky, watching the evening news every night. He liked Walter Cronkite.

Probably haunted by images, injuries and death, bombing of the Cassino Monastery and civilians, the carnage at the Rapido River crossing ambush, and the captured Germans in France. Loss of his friends and good soldiers. He didn't like killing.

His children have been busy raising their families nearby in the 60's and '70's and would assemble for holidays either in San Francisco or down on the Peninsula.

Meanwhile he would uneasily watch current events unfold, anti-war sentiment. Draft dodgers were the heroes. The barbarities of the Vietnam War. Countless brave men fighting for their country, drafted, coming home in body bags or severely injured mentally, emotionally and physically from the war. Civil unrest and war protests on college campuses.

Living near Haight Ashbury in San Francisco in the '60's. Hippies, free love, watching the kids perceive him as a warmonger, entitled to peace. 'Love not War' t-shirts, long disheveled hair, and 'Peace' signs.

——— ✶ ———

Figure 16 Frederic Bates Butler 1965

Figure 17 View from Grandparents home. Baker Beach 1970?

Author's Notes (Afterword)

I can't remember the last time I saw Granddaddy. I think he's buried at Golden Gate National Cemetery in San Bruno, California or somewhere in Colma. No one has been able to definitively tell me. Grandmommy is buried at Holy Cross Catholic Cemetery in the Town of Colma but with no marker.

I have nothing but some very soft faint fading memories of him. Like remembering our Grandparents driving their 1964 light blue Mercedes Benz 4-door Sedan slowly down our long hidden driveway in Los Altos to park in front of our house for a holiday dinner before alighting out of the car like royalty.

Or a picture I had of them once, standing proudly in front of that same blue Mercedes as they were in Europe taking delivery.

Or random thoughts of the coconut ice cream snowball desert with a lit candle in each that we enjoyed at their house after Christmas Eve dinner. I used to have pictures of us all around their long dining table with our cousins, aunts and uncles, smiling happily, posing with our desserts in the '60's and 70's.

I mean I have nothing tangible or material. No pictures. No heirlooms. Nothing I can physically hold on to other than what I can remember which seems to be slowly disappearing as time goes by.

Anything I may have had – like the fragile pieces of dinosaur egg from China wrapped in old crackling tissue paper, Grandmommy's six amethyst, well-used wine glasses (I had had them expertly sanded, ground down and restored), the folder Granddaddy had given me of parchment paper copies of all the American founding documents, collectively known as the Charters of Freedom, i.e. Declaration of Independence, the Constitution, Bill of Rights, etc..), the Childrens Bible with illustrations from my Holy Communion, or their hand carved, rosewood chair from China, Moms Japanese scrolls – turned to ashes in 1991 when my home burned down in the Oakland Hills firestorm.

And lastly, may I say I have never seen any of Granddaddy's or Grandmommy's personal or private papers, writings, letters, collections etc....

If given the privilege to view any of these at any point I would welcome the opportunity to do a deeper dive into his/her truth and perhaps create another expanded version of this short story. Until then, I have done my best with what I could piece together, publicly find and curate.

I know there is more somewhere and I look forward to discovering more about our grandparents.

If you have any comments, corrections or additional resources, please contact me at TaskForceButler.com. I welcome hearing from you.

So here we are.

To be continued...

Sources:

- Lewis H. Butler A Life of Public Service: Ploughshares Fund, California Tomorrow, Health Policy, HEW, the Environment, the Peace Corps Interviews conducted by Ann Lage in 2008-2009 Copyright © 2010 by The Regents of the University of California
- Task Force Butler: A Case Study in the Employment of an Ad Hoc Unit in Combat Operations, During Operation Dragoon, 1-30 August 1944 by Major Michael J. Volpe, 2007 Pickle partners publishing 2015 Lucknow books, from his sources R. Manning Ancell & Christine M. Miller The Biographical Dictionary of Flag Offices [59] The U.S. Armed Forces (Westport Greenwood Press 1996) 43
- Wikipedia 2024
- Command Missions – A Personal Story by Lt. General L.K. Truscott Jr., U.S.A., Pickle Partners Publishing © 2013 Original published in 1954
- CASSINO Portrait of a Battle by Fred Majdalany 1957 Longmans, Green & Co.
- Southern France "The U.S. Army Campaigns of World War II - U.S. Army Center of Military History brochure prepared by Jeffrey J. Clarke,
- "Calculated Risk", General Mark W. Clark © 1950
- Oral History Interview with General Frederic B. Butler by Raymond Henle, Director October 6, 1967 at San Francisco California For the Herbert Hoover Presidential Library West Branch Iowa and the Hoover Institution on War, Revolution

and Peace Stanford, California © Herbert Hoover Presidential Library Association, Inc.

- Operation Dragoon: Invasion of Southern France" Chris Rein PHD, Article WWII The National WWII Museum New Orleans
- Command of Honor, H. © Paul Jeffers 2008 Published by Penguin Books
- From the Alamo to the Riviera Warfare History Network www.warfarehistorynetwork.com/article/from-the-alamo-to-the-riviera
- Northwest Africa: Seizing the Initiative in the West By George F. Howe Library of Congress Catalog Card Number 57-60021 Pages 403-405, 490, 581
- Task Force Butler By Brig. General Frederic B. Butler inside of "The Operational History of the 117th Cavalry Reconnaissance Squadron (Mecs.) World War II U.S. Army

Index

The Author

Mary Patricia Henderson was born in Palo Alto California and is a 3rd generation Californian. She graduated from the University of California at Santa Barbara with B.A.'s in Environmental Studies and Economics. She enjoyed a successful, 30-year wall street career in finance, including owning her own boutique investment banking firm for over two decades. She lives in Sonoma County with her cat Buddy.

www.ingramcontent.com/pod-product-compliance
Lightning Source LLC
Chambersburg PA
CBHW051122300726

48981CB00021B/513/J